D1001365

THE
HOME FRONT

THE
HOME FRONT

Margaret Vandenburg

THE PERMANENT PRESS
Sag Harbor, NY 11963

For information, address:
  The Permanent Press
  4170 Noyac Road
  Sag Harbor, NY 11963
  www.thepermanentpress.com

Library of Congress Cataloging-in-Publication Data

Vandenburg, Margaret.
    The home front / Margaret Vandenburg.
        pages ; cm
    ISBN 978-1-57962-386-9
        1. Domestic fiction. I. Title.

PS3572.A647H66 2015
813'.54—dc23   2014041248

Printed in the United States of America.

for my mother

~ I ~

His cell phone rang the minute he left the trailer. He thought he might get used to it, flying drones one minute, chatting with his wife the next. Navigating the conflicting demands of combat and family life had never been easy. But oceans had always separated one from the other, not a forty-minute commute on US-95. Even he couldn't shift gears that fast. Then there was the trailer itself, the ultimate insult to what was left of his professional integrity. The fact that the Pentagon hadn't built an actual ground control station said it all. Everything was on the cheap since the downturn.

"Pick up some soy milk, will you? And a bag of potatoes for Max."

"Anything else?"

"Hurry home. The natives are restless."

Todd started the pickup and flicked on the lights. One thing he couldn't stand was daylight savings time. Millions of nine-to-fivers had to suffer for the four farmers left in the state of Nevada. Rose forced him to get tested for seasonal affective disorder, but it wasn't that. You didn't have to be sick to want to see a ray of sunshine after being glued to a computer console, especially since the day shift was really the night shift. When it was high noon at Creech Air Force Base it was just shy of midnight at Kandahar Airfield, the biggest hive of drones south of Kabul. He chased bad guys around dark deserts—hour after hour after hour—then drove home through a dark desert. If it weren't for weekends, he'd never see the light of day. Still, there was no use complaining. He tried to convince himself that virtual war beat freezing your hiney off in Afghanistan. Or worse yet, Pakistan. He was getting too old for heroics anyway.

Price Chopper was hopping. They were running a sale on hamburger packaged in red, white, and blue Styrofoam containers. Big beefy guys were stocking up, mostly bachelor types with plenty of pasty white buns in their carts. You are what you eat. Too bad Rose was on a health kick. Todd couldn't remember the last time she'd served a recognizable dinner, let alone one he could really sink his teeth into. Eating organically was like sucking meals through a straw, and his jaws ached for something more substantial than tofu and quinoa. At this rate his family would starve to death.

No use torturing himself wandering past the butcher. He made a beeline for the produce section. A dozen varieties of potatoes were heaped up in massive bins, none of which resembled the ones he ate growing up. The Idaho spuds were twice the normal size. They were beautiful, provided you liked the look of clones on steroids. Several new kinds of new potatoes were available in an astonishing spectrum of colors. Todd was tempted to try the bright purple ones, to see what color they were inside, but his son would blow a gasket. Max would only eat tan foods, the rounder the better, which put the kibosh on Rose's natural food fetish. Organic potatoes had unpredictable protrusions and unblinking eyes that completely disqualified them, even when mashed and reshaped into lumpy little balls. Rose had lots of tricks up her sleeve, but Max was no fool. The great virtue of genetically engineered vegetables was that they all shared a uniform shape and size. They were Max's version of comfort food.

Todd grabbed a bag of potatoes and headed for the checkout line. On the way he saw Dirk Brown cruising the beer aisle. His cart was filled with chips and salsa, enough to last a week. The sight of him made Todd feel nostalgic for the good old days when overseas deployments transformed beer-swilling cadets into fighter pilots. Ever since 9/11, the US Air Force funneled bozos like Brown into the domestic drone program. The sum of his qualifications was the capacity to wield joysticks like a third thumb, the ultimate bionic weapon. He was the video game equivalent of a pinball wizard. Todd knew full well the comparison dated him. In his day, pilots understood not only how to kill but also the gravity of killing. Brown was a hardcore gamer who thought drone warfare was a trip and a half. His exact words. He conducted himself more like a kid at a PlayStation than a warrior at the ready. Acne and all. It didn't help that virtual cockpits were designed to resemble game consoles to accommodate the likes of Dirk Brown. But a *Star Wars* aficionado does not a pilot make.

Todd ducked down the soda aisle. He frankly didn't know which was worse, commanding a squad of punks or running into them at the supermarket. Either way, professionalism was bound to erode. Not that Brown was to blame. Martial ethics relied on the imminent danger of getting your butt blown off. Flying drones from the air-conditioned comfort of a double-wide didn't exactly inspire valor and honor. For that matter, neither did running errands for your wife on the way home from what felt more like a desk job than active duty. His cell rang again.

"Where are you?"

"Like you don't know."

"Don't forget the milk."

She must have mounted a surveillance camera in his head. Either that or they'd been married long enough to read each other's minds. Even when he was stationed in Iraq, she always sensed when he was scheduled to fly particularly peril-ous missions. She'd call, pretending there was a medical emergency, so they could have phone sex. Marital telepathy. He missed those days. Living in the suburbs of Las Vegas certainly wasn't the life he'd envisioned at the Air Force Academy. Drones were a game changer, that's for sure, let alone autism. Maybe things would eventually calm down at home so he and Rose could pick up where they left off when Max was diagnosed. Their love was still there somewhere, underneath all the bullshit. Not that he blamed Max, poor kid. No one was to blame, which made it that much harder to swallow.

*   *   *

Max's diagnosis brought out the best in Rose. She rose to the occasion with all the passion of aroused motherhood. It brought out the worst of the worst in Todd. He felt helpless. Cheated. Angry. He took it out on the doctor, which was obnoxious but not unwarranted. Dr. Dillard never should have been allowed to practice medicine. He had the bedside manner of an accountant. Max started screaming the minute he laid eyes on him, a predictable enough response. He'd been screaming pretty much nonstop since roughly his third birthday. But he really let loose around Dr. Dillard. Neurological disorder notwithstanding, Max was a damned good judge of character.

Their regular pediatrician diagnosed one thing after another before admitting he was out of his league. Actually he probably just wanted to avoid being the bearer of bad news. They had to consult a specialist at University Medical Center in downtown Las Vegas. Fancy clinic, fancy doctors. Specialists in bad news. At 10:37 on Wednesday, March 4, Dr. Dillard ushered Rose and Todd into his office. Diagnosis day, or D-Day as Todd always referred to it, constituted the beginning of an interminably long, unthinkably costly siege with infinitesimal odds of prevailing against the enemy.

Dr. Dillard didn't look either one of them in the eye. He shook Todd's hand, but not Rose's, which pissed her off. He didn't apologize for being thirty-seven minutes late, which pissed Todd off. His desk was obscenely large and there was absolutely nothing on it except a pink folder. Pink. He peered at them over the top of his half glasses. The crown of his head had obviously been polished that morning, an affectation that further undermined his credibility. He opened the folder and delivered the diagnosis with deadpan certainty.

"Your son has autism."

"Are you sure?" Rose asked.

"His symptoms are unmistakable, Mrs. Barron."

They waited for him to continue. To clarify. To soften the blow with a favorable prognosis. A grandfather clock tolled the quarter hour. Todd checked his watch. 10:38. Everywhere he went, without thinking, he checked the accuracy of clocks, which were usually a minute or two off. Seven minutes was pathetic. This quack couldn't keep the proper time, let alone diagnose Max.

"You didn't even take a blood test," Todd said. "How can you be sure?"

"I can assure you that I examined him thoroughly."

"How serious is it?" Rose asked.

Dr. Dillard shuffled through the papers in his file, mostly hand-scribbled notes. All very scientific. "I regret to inform you that your son may never advance beyond the mental age of five or six." He closed the file.

"What about treatment options?" Rose asked.

"I'm a diagnostician, not a therapist."

"That's it?" Todd said. "You drop the bomb and then hightail it out of here?"

"The right diagnosis makes treatment possible."

"And the wrong diagnosis? What does the wrong diagnosis do?"

"I wouldn't know, Major Barron."

"Since you're so damn sure of yourself, let's pin down a number, Doctor. Five or six?"

"I beg your pardon."

"Any chance he might make it to seven?"

Dr. Dillard finally looked at him. They locked horns, staring each other down, while Rose tried to turn D-Day into

V-Day. By the time they left the doctor's office at 11:23, she had convinced herself that Max would eventually test off the spectrum, a term she had just learned and already used with a maternal authority that brooked no contradiction. Even Dr. Dillard stopped trying to tell her there was no known cure. The clock was tolling the half hour, seven fucking minutes fast, as Todd slammed the office door behind them. Together, he and Rose embodied the first two stages of grief—anger and denial. Acceptance would be a long time coming.

Rose threw herself into finding treatment options, which were still scarce in Nevada. Either the autism epidemic hadn't hit their fair state, or there weren't enough diagnosticians to deliver the bad news. The Internet became her doctor on call. Rose had never been one to surf the web, a completely unnecessary exercise with so many shopping malls nearby. She didn't even have a Facebook page. Everything changed after the diagnosis. Within a week, she had hundreds of friends, mostly mothers of children with autism and the occasional adult with Asperger syndrome. Official online sources propounded innumerable theories about the cause and treatment of the disorder. But none of them proved as instructive as her new Facebook friends.

The general consensus was that the best treatment program included a combination of Applied Behavior Analysis and Floortime therapies. Critics of ABA's unabashedly Pavlovian approach swore by Floortime, which was designed to ameliorate robotic behavior by developing emotional affect. Sorting out the pros and cons of each therapeutic approach was just the beginning. Board-certified therapists were hard to come by, not to mention outrageously expensive. Rose purchased instructional manuals online and started training herself. There was no way she could singlehandedly conduct the requisite seven hours of treatment per day. She tracked down local graduate students in psychology eager to work with Max for research credit and a nominal fee. Paying less for student therapists would leave more money to invest in the battery of baseline tests necessary to pinpoint his position on the spectrum. First Rose had to locate qualified specialists to administer the tests. Then she had to convince them that a month was too long to wait for an appointment. One after another seemingly insurmountable obstacle fell by the wayside. Within two weeks of Max's diagnosis, while Todd was still reeling from the shock, Rose had everything under control.

*   *   *

Rose had always been a take-charge kind of woman, the kind Todd's mother would have called a gal, not without a note of warning in her voice. She was working at a used car lot when they met. In sales. She was the only woman on the floor, needless to say. A woman is no more apt to buy a car from another woman than a man is. It's like having a female cardiologist, something you'd only do if you landed in an emergency room with no other option. The same is true in combat, for that matter. If you're relying on your buddies to bail you out of an ambush, the more testosterone the better. It's how everybody feels deep down, when their lives are on the line.

All the salesmen were busy helping other customers. Todd felt self-conscious when she approached him. He couldn't help noticing her legs, which was annoying at first. He was looking to buy a pickup, not pick up chicks.

"I need a truck," he said in self-defense.

"You're in luck," she said. "I've got a Chevy. A real beauty."

At first he thought she was joking. She sounded like a shyster in some B-movie about gangsters bootlegging behind used car fronts. Except that there was no cigar hanging out of the side of her mouth. Far from it. She wore bright red lipstick, a shade she only wore at work, it turns out. The job demanded a certain brassiness she performed on command.

It was like talking to a ventriloquist. She looked at him sideways, the way salesmen tend to look at you when they're sizing you up.

"I usually buy Fords."

"There's a first time for everything."

She dangled the keys just out of reach. Various parts of his body jumped when he looked at her outstretched hand. Her nail polish was several shades darker than her lipstick. He checked her fourth finger and she wasn't wearing a wedding ring. He bought the Chevy.

A year later, they were both wearing wedding rings. They lived in a rented duplex on the base the first four months of their marriage, a blissful period between tours in Iraq. One thing could be said for military life. It could prolong the honeymoon, provided you were lucky enough to have a wife who didn't punish you for overseas deployments. Todd's unit was gearing up for their second stint in Anbar Province. They were scheduled to fly out the day after Rose turned thirty. All the more reason to make it a birthday to remember.

There was no doubt in Todd's mind what Rose wished for every year she blew out the candles. She had a thing for sports cars. She thought it was the guys driving them she liked until she climbed into the driver's seat of a Jaguar. She may not have been the first person on the planet to get a speeding ticket test-driving a Jag. But you can bet the cop wasn't expecting to find a woman at the wheel. She never thought she'd actually own a sports car, especially now that she was married to an air force officer. Not exactly a lucrative profession, but a girl can dream. Out loud. A lot.

Todd couldn't see the appeal, frankly. Guys with four-wheel drive rarely appreciate the finer points of cars that can fit into the beds of their pickups. But he had to admit that the idea of his wife jamming a stick was worth the price of admission. She might have to settle for a used Corvette. Even then he'd practically have to mortgage his mother to come up with the money. Then an impossible deal on a Jaguar turned up. A steal, as Rose would have said in her used car lot days. A fellow officer at the base had to unload it quickly to stave off alimony lawyers. He was older but not too old to relish the idea of Todd's hot wife sitting in the driver's seat. His fantasy was simultaneously paternalistic and predatory. He was fond of Todd and wished him better luck than he had with women.

Miraculously, the Jaguar was black, Rose's favorite car color. Todd arranged to have his friend Bill deliver the present while he and Rose were eating birthday breakfast on the front porch. Bill was almost as excited as Todd. They fashioned a big red bow out of crepe paper and duct tape. News of the birthday present must have traveled across the base. Virtually all the guys had crushes on Rose. Inordinate numbers were taking strolls past the Barrons' house when the Jaguar rolled up, sleek and festive with that big bow on its hood.

Rose's eyes lit up when she caught sight of it, but the rest of her face remained impassive. Todd could see she was trying not to get her hopes up. It was her birthday and there was a Jaguar parked in her driveway. But girls like her didn't own sports cars. She had been raised with very modest expectations, which made surprising her easy and all the more enjoyable. Sometimes Todd wished he had pursued a more lucrative profession so she'd have that look on her face more often.

Bill jumped out and made a show of polishing the hood of the car with his sleeve. Then he joined the dozens of soldiers watching from the street. Rose kept looking back and forth, from the car to Todd's face, trying to figure out what was going on. Then all the guys started singing "Happy Birthday." Rose's eyes were flashing with excitement, but she still couldn't believe it.

"What's going on, Todd?"

"It's yours, baby. Happy birthday."

She threw her arms around him and all the guys started clapping and whistling. She was anything but prudish. Neither were they. But there was something so inherently sexual about the whole scene they started to disperse. Rose was blushing the color of the ribbon and she had never looked more beautiful. Todd had the impulse to pick her up and carry her to the car, but the gesture seemed out of place. This present was all about Rose being in the driver's seat, not him.

"Let's take her for a spin."

They ran out to the driveway, holding hands. Rose circled the car several times, dragging Todd along to look at every gleaming inch of her. She made him pet the hood ornament before they climbed in. When her bare legs touched the leather seat, she collapsed deep into its embrace. The car fit her like a glove.

Jaguars purr. When she turned the key in the ignition the engine vibrated smooth and steady and low to the ground, ready to pounce. She glanced over at Todd. He'd been watching her the whole time. His face looked like the car sounded. She caught sight of herself in the rearview mirror. She looked like the morning after, and they hadn't even left the driveway.

The security checkpoint guards must have also heard about the Jaguar. They waved her through the gate so she wouldn't have to slow down. Rose hit the highway already doing seventy. It felt like they were crawling along until they hit ninety. The highway shot straight as an arrow through the desert. Occasional trucks flew by, trailing quick blasts of wind in their wakes. Otherwise there was nothing but the open road and gas stations spaced at strategic intervals, like pit stops.

Todd couldn't take his eyes off Rose's hands on the wheel. She let it play through her fingers and then gripped it tightly. The alternating delicacy and mastery drove him crazy. He knew exactly what her hands felt like, taking control that way. Rose was keenly aware of the focus of Todd's attention. His thigh flexed every time she reached for the stick. Gripping the wheel was a way to steady herself, not the car, to postpone the inevitable as long as possible.

The faster they went, the less clear the distinction between car and driver. Everything was close at hand, intimate. She could flick every switch on the dash without taking her hands off the wheel. The proximity of the engine made every pumping piston feel like an extension of her body. The pavement itself was just inches away, within reach. They could feel it unfurl beneath them, miles and miles of open road with a magnetic vanishing point pulling them faster and farther, irresistibly.

Rose spotted the motel first, a classic roadhouse with flashing neon signage and several semis parked out back. She screeched into the parking lot and told Todd to wait in the car. She disappeared into the office, emerging a minute later with keys dangling from the forefinger of the same hand that had so recently gripped the stick. They spent the afternoon in Room 27.

The Jaguar never lost its luster. Rose was one of those women who could make everything new over and over again, just when Todd feared they might sink into a routine. Before the kids were born, they took road trips every chance they got. They stopped at sleazy motels to commemorate their maiden voyage. When Todd was deployed overseas, the Jag hibernated in the garage. Rose would sit in it periodically, to reminisce in its leather embrace, but driving without Todd felt masturbatory. It just made her feel more lonely.

When Maureen was born they still managed quickies on Saturday afternoons. They told babysitters they were spending the day at the mall. After Max's diagnosis, the Jag languished in the garage while they figured out the complicated logistics of his treatment. The expense was mind-boggling. They discussed the possibility of Rose getting a job to help pay for the army of neurologists, allergists, nutritionists, and therapists conscripted to rescue Max from his solipsistic fortress. A second income was out of the question. Rose would be needed full-time at home to coordinate the troops. Their son's brain was like a time bomb that would implode rather than explode if they couldn't manage to rewire its circuitry by the age of four or five. Every second counted.

Todd pored over spreadsheets, shifting nonexistent money back and forth to cover the cost of the rescue mission. They discussed cashing in Todd's pension plan, in spite of the penalties. Without a mortgage to leverage cash, their only option was to rack up credit card debt. Even then, bankruptcy was just a matter of time. They considered every option, no matter how farfetched, knowing full well as they schemed late into the night that there was one simple, tragic solution. The Jaguar.

Todd surprised Rose one Friday afternoon, coming home for lunch without calling ahead. He brought a babysitter along, a nurse from the base so Rose would agree to leave Max in capable hands for a few hours. His head-banging had gotten to the point where they couldn't trust him with regular sitters. The last one had called 9-1-1, scaring him half to death. With the exception of trips to doctors and pharmacies, Rose had been housebound for weeks, tending to Max.

That morning, Rose finished interviewing potential ABA therapists. She offered the job to Sasha, an abnormal psych graduate student with a little brother on the spectrum. The fact that Sasha didn't consider her brother abnormal convinced Rose she was right for the job. She was scheduled to begin work the following Monday, the official start date of Max's treatment program. All that remained was to set up the payment plan.

"Grab your purse," Todd said.

"Where are we going?" Rose asked.

"To the mall."

They revved up the Jag for one last vertiginous spree on the open road. They raced by one sleazy motel after another without even slowing down. Todd couldn't tell if she was angry or just too sad to consummate the trip. When they got back home, Rose parked out front. She left the keys in the ignition. They hadn't talked about a thing, had just driven to the vanishing point and back in silence. Her sixth sense had already relinquished the Jaguar.

"You'll have to go without me," she said. "I can't bear it."

It was almost five and the dealership would be closing for the day. Todd climbed out of the passenger seat for the last time. He had prepared a speech about how selling the car didn't mean forfeiting the feelings attached to it. Actually naming the feelings would be impossible, but Rose would know what he meant. She was already halfway across the lawn. He called her name and she disappeared into the house, pretending not to hear. She hadn't even said good-bye to the hood ornament.

*   *   *

Max always lined up his potatoes in two rows of four. Todd appreciated the military precision of the configuration. He knew he shouldn't. There was something terribly wrong with a boy who would only eat round, tan foods. Most of Max's dinner was on the floor halfway across the room. Green beans were not tan. Tofu steaks were not round. Rose refused to stop dishing a full meal onto his plate, no matter where it ended up. Max's behavioral therapist insisted that giving in to his whims would reinforce them, and all would be lost. Todd understood this to mean they were engaged in a battle of wills. Max versus everybody else. He couldn't help admiring his son's determination. It had been months since he'd eaten anything that wasn't round and tan.

Everyone was pretending they were a perfectly normal family eating a perfectly normal dinner. Rose was helping herself to another gooey dollop of tofu surprise. Todd was politely refusing seconds, having already devoured a Big Mac and fries on the way home from work. A preemptive strike. Maureen was clamoring for dessert. Once she finished her so-called meal there was nothing to do but badger her parents. Teasing her younger brother was no fun. He barely knew she existed.

"What's for dessert?"

"I already told you," Rose said. "Carob sorbet."

"Can I watch videos until you guys finish eating?"

"How many times do I have to say no, young lady?"

Maureen was sick and tired of her mother's random rules. She turned to her father, hoping she could leverage him more effectively. In her experience, fathers were pushovers. They weren't around enough to keep track of all the regulations laid down by mothers, who apparently had nothing better to do than sit home all day terrorizing their children. Fathers went to work and earned what they called a living, which gave them the right to be grumpy when they got home.

"Daddy?"

"You heard your mother."

"I'm bored."

"Smart people don't get bored."

"What do they do?"

"They make conversation."

"Yada yada yada."

"Tell us about your day at school."

Todd was careful to pay as much attention as possible to Maureen. Having an autistic brother was like sharing the nest with a gorilla. Miraculously, she didn't seem to mind all that much. She was a classic eldest child whose ego was even bigger than the gorilla. Rose attributed it to the fact that Maureen was a Leo. Max was a Sagittarius, but either autism or his rising sign must have eclipsed his sunny disposition. Given the circumstances, their daughter was remarkably well-adjusted. She tripped off to school without throwing tantrums. She played with her dolls without ripping their heads off. She ate her supper without herding it into two rows of four.

"Anne's dad came to talk about his job," Maureen said.

"That's nice," Rose said. "What does he do?"

"He's a plumber."

"A noble profession," Todd said.

"What does that mean?"

"Your father was joking."

"No I wasn't."

"He fixes toilets."

"I rest my case," Todd said. "What could be more noble than that?"

"What do you do at work, Daddy?"

Before Max's diagnosis, Todd dreaded the day his children would grow old enough to ask this question. Afterward, he feared that Max might never develop the language skills necessary to ask it. In any case, the answer was classified top secret.

"Everything but fix toilets. We bring Anne's dad in for that."

"What about dripping faucets?"

"Yup. That's my job."

"For heaven sake, Todd," Rose said. "Do you want Maureen to tell her friends at school you fix faucets for a living?"

"Why not? Like I said. It's a noble profession."

"Not as noble as defending your country."

Todd shot Rose one of their coded parental looks, which, in layman's terms, meant what's your goddamned problem. Rose knew better. She was usually a model military wife, steering clear of her husband's profession, which was way too explosive for table talk. Her capacity to dredge up innocuous topics of conversation was unparalleled. But once in a while she buckled under pressure, especially when they'd already exhausted their old standbys during the salad course.

There were only so many times you could talk about Max's sessions with his behavioral therapist. They had discussed what they hoped was a breakthrough for the past two weeks, analyzing it from every possible angle. Max had suddenly started not only noticing but miraculously grabbing a kaleidoscope ball Sasha had ordered online from the autistic version of ToysЯUs. You'd have thought he'd learned how to play catch, they were so excited. Then, just as abruptly, he was oblivious to the ball. Sasha remained sanguine. Two steps forward and one step back. Rose worked through her disappointment with her Facebook friends. Todd was still devastated.

The further they immersed themselves in the PCA lifestyle—Parents of Children with Autism—the less there was to talk about. An old friend had called that morning, inviting them to spend the weekend at their cabin, but Rose decided against mentioning it. No need to tempt Todd with an invitation they couldn't possibly accept. Gossiping about the extended family used to be mildly entertaining, especially Max and Maureen's quirky grandparents. But they had stopped visiting even before Max's diagnosis, and since then they rarely called. Rose's father said he was getting too old to travel. He wasn't too old to bowl two nights a week, presumably because no one in the league was autistic. Rose was too relieved to call his bluff. Every visit felt like a prolonged accusation in the guise of trying to be helpful. Her father in particular meted out advice like an implacable headmaster. All Max needed was some good old-fashioned discipline. If his mother couldn't control him, Todd should haul out the strap. Todd's parents were even worse. They flat out didn't believe in autism. It was a fad, not an epidemic. Talk about a conversation stopper.

Rose's comments about Todd's mysterious profession, in all its patriotic glory, hung in the air. She mimed a chastened expression to signal her willingness to drop the subject, even though the idea that she was threatening national security was patently ridiculous. Todd could be such a control freak sometimes, especially lately when Max's condition made him feel so out of control. He pretended to ignore Rose's body language, the better to deflect Maureen's attention. They both assumed their table talk was too generic to arouse her curiosity, more like something you'd hear in civics class than a deep dark family secret. But Maureen was a classic eldest child in more ways than one. She was precocious, above all, in her ability to manipulate family dynamics, usually to her advantage. When she saw an opening, she pounced on it.

"Matt says you kill people for a living," Maureen said.

"Who's Matt?"

"My nap partner."

"Your nap partner is a boy?"

"Daddy doesn't kill people," Rose said. "He protects our country against bad guys."

"He doesn't kill them?"

"Only the bad guys."

And sometimes civilians. And sometimes their children. It hadn't been a good day at the office. Not that it ultimately mattered a whole hell of a lot in present company. The answer to the innocuous question—How was work?—could never be innocuous enough to share with his kids. What could he say? *It was great. I killed three al Qaeda operatives.* And that was a good day.

"How can you tell the difference, Daddy?"

Every other night that week, Todd would have shrugged off the whole misguided conversation. His defenses were down. He tried not to slam his fork down too hard, but everyone except Max jumped anyway.

"I'll get the dessert," Todd said.

His napkin dropped to the floor as he stood up. Rose smiled at Maureen, pretending nothing was happening as she bent over to retrieve the napkin. Maureen smiled back, hoping to avoid getting into trouble for asking too many questions. Neither of them noticed that Max was watching his father storm out of the room. His face was blank, but his eyes were intently focused.

*   *   *

Technically it wasn't Todd's fault, which made little or no difference. He was the flight commander, such as it was, but not the pilot of the actual plane, which wasn't actually a

~ 23 ~

plane. It was a drone and Brown was in a virtual rather than real cockpit. The official report cited a control glitch, which was nominally responsible for identifying the wrong target. Whether the error was human or technological remained unspecified, if not obscured. One way or the other, accountability was a real problem in drone warfare. All the more reason for Todd to guard against pretending that all of these contingencies let him off the hook. They made little difference to him and no difference to the dead Afghan family.

Todd's squadron spent most of their time tracking down targets. Sensor zooms were so powerful they could read license plates from optimum cruising altitude, miles above unsuspecting drivers. Their computers automatically ran checks to see if the cars and trucks in question had been involved in hostile encounters. These high-tech innovations were indispensable. The enemy didn't bother wearing uniforms, let alone deign to drive official military vehicles. Even ambulances had been commandeered by sectarian militia. Surveillance drones could be preprogrammed to monitor potentially high-value targets. But armed Predators and Reapers still needed pilots, guys like Brown pulling triggers from the safety of air-conditioned trailers almost 8,000 miles from the nearest potential enemy. The air force made a big deal of calling them remotely piloted aircraft rather than drones, as though the latter term were misleading and derogatory. Todd was a straight shooter. He called a spade a spade and figured drones by any other name were still drones.

Todd had done his best to train his pilots to be battle ready. None of them had ever seen real action. This was the new air force. If virtual warfare required the ability to walk and chew gum at the same time, they were ready enough to fly drones. Todd had to admit they were more adept at processing information than he was. They could simultaneously monitor up to seven computer screens, assessing flight coordinates, real-time video feeds, infrared imaging, crosshair targets, and constant streams of intelligence from boots on the ground. But they were still more like professional multitaskers than real pilots. Traditional pilots also made mistakes from time to time. Civilians still accounted for a significant number of casualties in the war on terror. But with so much logistical information at their fingertips, virtual pilots should have been better equipped to steer clear of innocent bystanders.

Todd had spent the afternoon floating from one virtual cockpit to the next, feeling more like a systems analyst than an air force officer. The army may have been willing to let Nintendo nerds fly armed Predators, but USAF drone squads were supervised by seasoned pilots like himself. After several hours of routine surveillance, they had finally been tasked with an actual combat mission. A marine platoon in the Nawa District needed aerial support. Nobody on the ground had been able to pinpoint the source of the threat that was pounding Alpha Company with short-range missiles. If a specific target was identified by the time they heard the drones overhead, they'd retreat and let Reapers finish the job with laser-guided bombs. At the very least, Todd's squadron could provide aerial intelligence.

Often as not, there were too many civilians in the vicinity to accommodate air strikes, even in the mountainous regions of Afghanistan and Pakistan. Todd never relied exclusively on ground intelligence to make this determination. Or computer intelligence, for that matter. A Predator had eyes in the back of its head, quite literally. If you made judicious use of technology, virtual combat could actually save innocent lives. But only if you partnered with drones, augmenting their intelligence with your own. Distinguishing between enemy combatants and civilians was easier said than done, especially when suicide bombers wore burqas and terrorist cells were housed in family homes.

Visibility couldn't have been better, especially since the local time was 0700 hours. Todd and his squad had been working late almost every day since the recent surge in drone strikes. They were used to watching Afghans eat dinner and bed down for the night. Longer shifts meant they also watched them get up and get going in the morning. Senior al Qaeda leaders didn't necessarily keep regular hours. But their wives and children did, as did the families of Taliban warlords in tribal areas, everyday people living everyday lives under constant surveillance.

Spending more time cooped up in the trailer obviously had its downside. But there was one big payoff. The squad actually got to see more action. Even at night infrared sensors made everything visible in an incandescent, ghostly way. Surprisingly few dark places were left on the map anyway, given the ubiquity of electricity. But nocturnal surveillance still paled in comparison with what they saw in the early morning light. When the sun started rising over mountain peaks, they switched from infrared to regular high-resolution cameras. The landscape was breathtaking, a femme fatale of natural beauty whose countless cliffs and gullies provided cover for enemy combatants. Surveilling mile after mile of undifferentiated desert in southern Afghanistan, boredom blunted their vigilance. Here, the danger was sensory overload. There was almost too much to take in.

Spring was the only time of year the Sulaiman Mountains seemed to call a truce with nature. It was deceptive, of course, like everything else in the region. Wildflowers sprouted from rocky soil in the wake of receding snow banks. They scarcely had time to bloom before the punishing suns of summer withered their roots. The more inhospitable the landscape, the better it suited militants and terrorists. No one saw them resume their positions in bunkers concealed in caves on the craggy peaks. They seemed to thaw along with the snow, sprouting like sinister flowers from the landscape itself, ready to resume the fight each spring.

Todd was supervising Poindexter, the weakest pilot in the squadron, when Kucher let out a whoop. He had a keen eye and almost always identified visual anomalies before anyone else.

"There they are," Kucher said.

Todd rushed over to his cubicle just in time to see a cluster of helmets hunkered down in a makeshift dugout. What looked like tiny puffs of smoke kept obscuring their location. On the ground, the puffs were lethal mortar blasts landing dangerously close to a squad of marines.

"Verify the coordinates of the rest of the platoon," Todd ordered.

"They're way out of range behind that ridge, Major Barron."

"Any word on the origin of the threat?"

"It's coming in now."

A high mountain village zoomed into view. Dusty footpaths connected a dozen stone dwellings. Suspicious dark specks traversed the adjacent hillside. A third monitor scoped them. A herd of goats scattered, spooked by concussive shell fire blasting from a house on the southern perimeter of the village.

"Last one there is a rotten egg," Brown said.

Brown was the class clown. Todd could tell from his tone of voice that he was closing in on the target. He couldn't resist hotdogging, even though it violated regulations. Unless someone kept an eye on him, he performed celebratory dances in his chair every time he scored a hit. This time he cut it short without being reprimanded. The customary hooting and hollering wasn't forthcoming either. Todd thought maybe Brown was finally starting to grow up.

"Fuck!"

Brown jumped to his feet and stared wild-eyed at his monitor.

"What's going on?"

Todd rushed over to Brown's cubicle. The words *enemy target* were still flashing on the weapons activation screen. A laser-guided Hellfire missile had wasted an Afghan family. A mother's shredded burqa smoldered in the wreckage. One after another monitor zoomed in on miniature body parts slick with blood. A howling dog had survived the explosion, but nothing and no one else. Mortar fire still streamed from the house on the southern perimeter. Some glitch somewhere had misidentified the target.

*   *   *

Todd recovered his equilibrium in time to put the kids to bed. Rose had already read bedtime stories. Todd covered the swing shift, tucking them in a second time to make sure everyone understood that they were one big happy family. Maureen always wanted him to read another story, but he hated children's books. They were either saccharine or preachy. Even Dr. Seuss, who was refreshingly imaginative, couldn't resist slipping in Marxist propaganda every chance he got. If Yertle the Turtle hadn't toppled the tyrant tortoise, the pond probably would have spawned wage slaves rather than polly-wogs. Enough already.

Todd preferred making up his own stories. Maureen didn't object as long as they had plenty of ribbons and bows in them. She loved carriages and ballrooms and princes and princesses in gowns with lots of ribbons and bows, none of which Todd felt qualified to weave into a plausible plot. But every time his tales strayed too far away from Disneyland, she pouted. He was forced to do the best he could with ribbons and bows. Fortunately, they were portable and surprisingly versatile.

"Once upon a time there was a piece of linguine named Sam."

"Daddy!"

"What?"

"You promised."

"Don't worry. This particular piece of linguine had a big bow tie."

"Make him a girl."

"Okay. Once upon a time there was a lovely linguine named Samantha with a big beautiful bow in her hair."

"Linguine doesn't have hair."

"Who says? Mom just serves the bald kind."

Maureen rolled her eyes. She was amused but uncertain whether linguine belonged in the realm of conventional make-believe.

"What kind of hair?" she asked.

"Very, very straight hair. Until you cook it, of course. Then it gets curly."

Todd could see that Maureen was on the verge of rejecting his story. It wouldn't have been the first time. She kept him on a short leash, making improvisation all the more challenging. He had to include just enough fairy tale schlock to disguise his unorthodox flights of fancy.

"Did I mention that the bow was red? And that Samantha wore it even in bed?"

Red was Maureen's favorite color. This reassuring detail seemed to compensate for the fact that the bow wasn't attached to a silk or, better yet, satin gown. She was also a sucker for rhymes, like every other child on the planet. Pulling her covers up to her chin, she finally settled into the tale.

"One day Samantha was out riding her big black stallion—"

"Daddy!"

"Now what?"

"Kings ride stallions. White ones."

"Silly me."

Todd made a show of bonking his head with the heel of his hand, which elicited the desired response. Maureen giggled and squirmed with delight. She loved correcting her father, which was the only reason she tolerated his boring digressions.

"Samantha was out riding her Shetland pony—sidesaddle, of course—when all of a sudden a renegade band of bow tie pastas kidnapped her and locked her in a tower."

"What does renegade mean?"

"Good question. Let's ask Puff."

Todd picked up one of Maureen's menagerie of stuffed animals. The bed was littered with them. So were the window-sills and the floor, along with millions of other tchotchkes and discarded pieces of clothing. Maureen was a regular Pig-Pen. Todd would never understand how a child with such an appetite for orderly bedtime stories could tolerate such a mess. It drove him crazy, but Rose no longer let him intervene. Max's psychiatrist insisted that children's bedrooms were their own personal domain. As long as Maureen didn't trash the rest of the house, her slovenly habits were beyond her father's juris-diction. Todd's only recourse was to shut her bedroom door, which usually meant kicking several toys out of the way.

Puff was a pink unicorn with a silky white mane. Todd regretted the choice. He hated unicorns, which were vaguely lewd and embarrassing. Puff bobbed up and down in his hand as he spoke in a high-pitched voice.

"Renegade means they're outlaws. Rogues with their own ideas about how to run the show."

"I don't like them."

"They don't care if you like them," Todd said in his normal voice.

"They're the bad guys?"

"They're the renegade guys."

Maureen yawned. Complexity bored her. If a knight in shining armor didn't show up soon, she'd fall asleep in pro-test. Nine nights out of ten, lack of interest forced Todd to conclude his tales abruptly, or not at all.

"Their king—His Majesty the Imperial Bow Tie Pasta—"

Maureen perked up a little.

"—decreed that Samantha be sent to the guillotine."

"Why?"

"To sever her big red bow from her lovely linguine body. So she'd look like them."

"I don't like this story."

"Would you like it if I told you the king's son, the Prince of Bow Ties, thought Samantha was beautiful the way she was?"

"Maybe."

"He rescued her from the tower and they galloped away on his bright white stallion."

"And they lived happily ever after," Maureen whispered. She rolled over and buried her face in her pillow.

"Actually, the king dispatched his knights in hot pursuit," Todd said urgently. But it was too late. His audience had already taken refuge in la-la land. The whole point of bedtime stories was to make children feel safe enough to go to sleep. But he was always disappointed when Maureen dozed off before he finished. It meant he would never find out what happened, whether a linguine and a bow tie pasta could ever really live happily ever after in Neverland, or whether they would be forced to flee to San Francisco to escape censure. He was left hanging, as usual, suspended in the inconclusive uniformity of fairy tale endings.

He kissed his daughter on the forehead and made for the door, tripping over one of her Barbie dolls on the way out. It skittered across the floor into the hallway. Fortunately, there was no need to tiptoe around Maureen. She slept as soundly as he did. The Barbie just missed hitting a line of trucks leading to Max's bedroom. There would be hell to pay if even one of them was disturbed. Max had a virtual tape measurer in his mind. Every single truck was in precisely the same place every single night. There was something preordained about their positions, something fixed and immutable, as though Max communed with an omniscient authority that punished the slightest deviation. Todd had stepped over them so many times he could have done it with his eyes closed. The entire family had been inducted into Max's secret universe, at least to the extent that they religiously avoided breaking its sacred laws.

The diesel flatbed always led the way. It was bigger and brighter than the rest of the trucks. Todd wondered how a boy who cringed from all but tan foods could tolerate a fire-engine red flatbed. The only plausible explanation was proffered by his behavioral therapist. Sasha seemed to know Max better than his parents did. Rose accepted this as a matter of course. Back in the day, she had read and admired Hillary Clinton's *It Takes a Village*. But consulting with a virtual stranger to understand his son bothered Todd. The last thing he needed was politicians telling him how to raise his kids. Let alone therapists.

According to Sasha's latest theory, Max's rituals were designed to ward off change, a common enough fear exacerbated but not caused by autism. She was adamant about the fact that he was just like everyone else, only more so. She pretended to ground her theories in demonstrable evidence. Max's favorite trucks were a case in point. Having received them as gifts on or before his third birthday, prior to the onset of his symptoms, he took their vibrant colors for granted. To say they were his favorite toys was the kind of gargantuan understatement only possible in an autistic household. The mere sight of a new truck threw Max into annihilation mode. Even if they were tan, he smashed them against the wall and hammered their wheels off. His parents finally stopped trying to give him new toys for Christmas. Presents were like booby traps, so much so that even watching his sister open gifts terrorized him. His psychic fortress was erected to eliminate the element of surprise. All he wanted for Christmas was to be left alone.

With one inexplicable exception, Max's trucks were always lined up from biggest to smallest. Even Sasha couldn't figure out why a pickup half the size of the next truck came second in line. Todd liked to think it was because he drove a Chevy pickup. He was desperate for even a pathological connection with his son. Sasha counseled against reinforcing autistic as opposed to ostensibly normal vocabularies. Rose complied with characteristic enthusiasm, never acknowledging Max's private languages. Todd complied judiciously. In mixed company, he pretended to ignore Max's idiosyncratic sign systems. When they were alone, he tried to decode them.

Exactly one inch separated the back fender of one truck from the front of the next. Max's spatial precision was astonishing. Rose was already predicting a career in engineering. Everyone in the autism community was forever talking about Temple Grandin, their patron saint. You didn't have to make eye contact with strangers, or even your parents, to design livestock corrals. Something to look forward to, a son whose crowning achievement was figuring out how to slaughter animals without scaring them half to death. Todd knew he had no right to be skeptical, a man who killed other men for a living.

Last in line was an oil truck. Todd's personal favorite. Growing up in Los Angeles, kids used to pump their fists up and down trying to get truckers to blow their big throaty horns. By far the most responsive were the tank truck drivers. They owned the road and liked the sounds of their own voices. Todd was surprised the oil truck wasn't closer to the front. It was the only truck with a round body. Other mysterious criteria must have prevailed, trumping its shape. The only thing Max loved more than circles were dust motes, quite possibly because they swirled round and round and round. He could watch them for hours, floating in shafts of sunlight, but only in the living room with the curtains drawn halfway. More or less sent him into paroxysms of blind rage.

Max's rituals were unbelievably precise and complex. As long as everything was just so—calibrated to fractions of inches and other less tangible units of measurement known only to himself—he spent quiet hours at a time, arranging his toys into elaborate, soothing patterns. Repeating sounds and gestures to block out the threat of everything random and uncontrollable. And, most recently, murmuring sequences of numbers related in ways Todd could scarcely fathom. Sasha was trying to introduce Max to a whole new range of educational toys designed to discover his native languages. He was obviously very smart, underneath all that obsessive-compulsive behavior, quite possibly a prodigy. They say Einstein was on the spectrum as a boy.

Talk about magical thinking. The last thing Max needed was the pressure of unreasonable expectations. Rose was the worst offender. Every time he glanced in her direction she was convinced they'd made eye contact. When he growled, which he did routinely for no apparent reason, she claimed she could distinguish actual words, even phrases. Her latest fantasy conviction was that he had actually learned to wave hello and good-bye. Todd was hard-pressed to tell the difference between waving and flapping, their son's favorite form of stimming. It seemed incredible that children with autism from Las Vegas to Beijing all seemed to speak the same language, flapping their arms when they were agitated by too much noise, too many people too close, too much of everything everywhere. The fact that Max's waves hello and good-bye coincided with onslaughts of excessive stimulation did nothing to dampen Rose's enthusiasm. She waved back, encouraging Todd to do the same. Sometimes he actually did it to keep the peace, feeling half mad for indulging her delusions.

He called her Pollyanna behind her back, muttering to himself to bolster his own more pragmatic approach. In turn, Rose accused Todd of being negative. She and her Facebook friends complained about their husbands almost as much as they compared notes on treatment options. Overall, men were a cynical lot. They pretended to be reasonable when in fact they were pessimistic. They dwelled on the past rather than looking to the future. Todd was especially prone to this particular vice. What if they hadn't vaccinated Max for measles? What if he hadn't taken six rounds of antibiotics between his first and second birthdays? What if his doctor hadn't ignored the early warning signs? According to Todd, their former pediatrician might as well have been an axe murderer. What was done was done.

Before Max's diagnosis, Rose and Todd seldom fought. When they did it was over money or the antics of one of their in-laws. After his diagnosis, their families deserted them and every dollar was invested in Max's treatment, case closed. So they argued about Max's prognosis instead. Secretly, Todd wasn't as negative as he appeared to be. But someone had to occupy that position, to maintain the balance between good cop and bad cop that was the foundation of every sound marriage. There was also an element of self-defense in the posture of the curmudgeon. Underneath it all, Todd was just as vulnerable to disappointment as Rose. The tough air force officer routine was part of a lifelong effort to ward off the agony of feeling too much too often, not unlike his son.

He opened Max's bedroom door tentatively. Light from the hallway barely illuminated the bed. Todd thought he detected a flurry of arm flapping. But when he walked into the room, everything was as perfectly still as only an autistic child's room can be still, pregnant with the immanence of alternate realities. Max was already asleep. Or he was coma-tose, lost in another world far preferable to the one his family inhabited. Or he was playing possum, something they had only recently discovered he did to elude human contact. You never knew with Max. Trying to figure him out was like trying to decipher the Rosetta Stone's monolithic muteness. Half of the doctors they consulted encouraged them to learn Max's multiple foreign languages. Rituals and even stimming were a kind of vocabulary. Facial expressions, or lack thereof, could speak volumes, they said. The other half told them to ignore or even discourage these other languages, to force him to communicate with words.

There were so many theories Todd had lost track of them all. He started relying on his instincts instead. He tried to meet his son halfway, with mixed results. Sometimes Max seemed to reciprocate, responding in oblique ways that might have seemed random to the untrained eye. Hide and seek was the only game he deigned to play with his sister, one entirely in keeping with his desire to disappear. Paradoxically, this impulse to hide provided a common language. Todd would tease Ralph and Harry, Max's favorite stuffed animals, about sneaking into his bedroom closet. Lo and behold, three weeks later, Todd would find Harry nestled behind sweaters on the bottom shelf. As suspicious as he was of Rose's magical thinking, he clung to the possibility that Max had placed him there, however belatedly, for a reason. Even Todd couldn't bear the thought that the lines of communication were permanently shut down.

Once upon a time their son had been perfectly normal. He used to play with his trucks instead of obsessing over them. He used to let his father tuck him in. What if his regression was reversible? There was mounting clinical evidence that what was done could be undone. What if he was still in there somewhere, hiding? Come out, come out, wherever you are.

*   *   *

Somebody comes into the room. They're too big and too loud. The light goes on. He closes his eyes and it goes off. If he doesn't move no one can see him. He can still hear something but it isn't really there as long as he isn't. After a while the door shuts and he can't even hear what isn't there.

~ II ~

Rose could hear them all the way from the kitchen. Every once in a while Max made a noise, usually a whimper. The occasional piercing cry. But mostly she heard Sasha walking him through ABA exercises, using the singsong voice people reserved for toddlers. Children like Max supposedly thrived on consistency. It made them feel safe. Sasha repeated the same phrases in the same lilting cadence session after session. Week after week. Month after month. Todd called it ABBT. Applied Behavior Baby Talk. It drove him crazy. They had both refused to talk down to Maureen, using their regular adult voices even when she was an infant. Then Max came along and all bets were off. If squeaking like Mickey Mouse was the only way to attract his attention, so be it.

"Make a match, Max," Sasha said.

Max let out a scream.

"Make a match, Max."

Something crashed to the floor. Hopefully it was a chair, not a person, something that wouldn't need to be rushed to the emergency room. The den had been transformed into what Sasha called a playroom, as though behavioral therapy were a kind of game that could be fun. It was more like a war zone. Rose swore she'd never turn into one of those helicopter mothers with nothing better to do than fret over their children. Grunting and a series of thumps weakened her resolve. Either Max was hitting Sasha or kicking the legs of his chair. It sounded more like flesh than wood on impact. Sasha's voice never skipped a beat, even under siege.

"Make a match, Max."

Rose opened the door. Sasha turned to smile at her, fending off Max's fists without otherwise acknowledging the attack. He continued pummeling her, oblivious to his mother's appearance at the door. He didn't even seem consciously aware of Sasha's presence in the room. His eyes were glazed over, staring at the window. His arms moved robotically, as though remotely controlled, if any measure of control could be assigned to such disembodied violence.

"Make a match, Max."

Sasha grabbed Max's left hand and guided it over to one of two apples on the play station, a table designed specifically for behavioral exercises. A lone orange, pocked with teeth marks, rolled onto the floor. The props were round, in deference to Max's obsession with circles and spheres, but brightly colored. Sasha was trying to expand his palette of acceptable colors.

Max refused to pick up the apple. Rose wondered whether it even registered in his consciousness. Sasha never bothered with such fine distinctions. What mattered was the task at hand. She continued grasping Max's hand while she picked up one apple and placed it next to the other.

"Good boy, Max. You matched the apples!"

Rose admired Sasha's tenacity. She was one tough cookie. At the same time, she could be fun loving and warm. In bygone days, she would have been everybody's favorite Girl Scout leader. Even Max had taken to her almost instantaneously, in spite of the fact that she was an unrelenting taskmaster. Once in a while he actually wandered into the playroom when he heard her car in the driveway. When he wasn't pulverizing her, he could be remarkably cooperative. Not that he had a choice. Max had learned that he could never escape completing an exercise. If he refused to make a match several times in a row, Sasha would grab his hand

and guide him through the motions. She preferred to call this modeling rather than forcing him to comply. One way or another, if they were engaged in a battle of wills, he had met his match.

"You're such a good boy, you get to play with your toys."

At first Rose thought Max actually understood Sasha. For a moment he looked like any other kid, liberated from homework, rushing across the room to play with his favorite toys. He ran right past them and plopped down at the far edge of the Oriental rug, where the fringe was frayed from overuse. He pinched one string after another between his tiny fingers, twisting them tight and then laying them straight and flat against the wood floor. Such precision and delicacy seemed impossible in a little boy.

Sasha was unimpressed. She lifted him up and walked him over to where Captain America reclined next to a stack of Legos.

"With your toys, Max," Sasha said. "Play with your toys."

Max raised a fist. Sasha ducked in time and Legos went flying across the room. He might have been expressing anger or excitement. It was hard to tell. His expression remained as blank as before except that now he was staring at the rug instead of the window. By the time Sasha and Rose gathered up the Legos, he was back at the fringe, pinching and twisting.

Rose would have conceded the point. She had grown accustomed to Max's more innocuous stimming rituals. She vaguely remembered that even Maureen had fiddled with the carpet at that age. Distinguishing the line between normal and compulsive behavior was becoming increasingly difficult.

"Good boys play with their toys," Sasha said.

She hauled him across the room three times before he gave up on the rug and started playing with Captain America. In a manner of speaking. He held the action figure immobile on his lap, tracing the outline of the lone star emblazoned on its chest, over and over and over. Apparently this was good enough for Sasha, who drew a liberal line between stimming and playing as long as toys were involved. She checked her watch. They'd take a five-minute recess and then get back to work at the play station.

Sasha retrieved her logbook and started recording the results of the match game. *Ten tries, six of them successful without assistance.* Rose sat next to her on a beanbag chair. Periodically, she checked in on Max's progress. ABA guidelines counseled against it, but Sasha had an open door policy. She wanted parents to be as involved as possible in the therapeutic process.

Applied Behavior Analysis was like the Bible. Its teachings sparked controversy, but it was inescapably canonical. Even Floortime was developed in the spirit of the Protestant Reformation, innovative only insofar as it rejected ABA's fundamentally Pavlovian approach. Sasha was trained in both programs. Though each had its virtues, utilizing both simultaneously would just confuse Max. So Rose employed the more imaginative techniques of Floortime, while Sasha stuck with ABA's more mechanical methodology. Few parents had the stomach to conduct behavioral therapy sessions. They required a velvet fist better suited to therapists than family members.

"He's less agitated than yesterday," Rose said.

"But less focused," Sasha said. "He seems tired."

"We were up half the night."

"Any particular reason?"

"Not that I can think of. Everything was fine when Todd tucked him in."

"Any variation in their routine?"

"Of course not."

"Are you sure? This could be important."

Rose found it virtually impossible to focus on flaws in their regimen. Even if she managed to pinpoint the causes of Max's tantrums, dwelling on them seemed to invite negative energy, which she couldn't afford to do. Todd accused her of being Pollyanna. But in reality she was prone to depression, a fact she did everything in her power to disguise even from herself. Had her father not been an alcoholic, she might have self-medicated with booze. Instead, she kept the abyss at bay with almost manic optimism. She had inherited this technique from her mother, a chronic Midwesterner with superhuman powers of repression and denial. It had never let her down before, and she wasn't about to let a little thing like autism rain on her parade. She reviewed Max's bedtime routine and chose the most upbeat explanation for his agitation.

"I had to wash his sheets. But that hasn't set him off for months now."

"When was the last time you washed them?"

"Day before yesterday."

"Why so often?"

"He had an accident during nap time."

"An accident or an incident?"

"What do you mean?"

"He may have done it on purpose." Sasha recorded the incident in her notebook as she spoke. "Kids can get pretty attached to their own smells. Like animals marking their territory. It probably makes them feel safe."

"An accident," Rose said, unconsciously gravitating toward the more positive alternative.

"Try using unscented detergent. Less of a shock to his system."

"That should do the trick."

"It might."

"It will," Rose said, somewhat more adamantly than she had intended.

Sasha looked up from her notebook. "It's certainly worth a try, one way or the other. But don't get your hopes up too high."

Part of Sasha's job was managing parental expectations, boosting morale without making false promises. She struggled with this balance herself, especially in a profession that focused on pathology rather than wellness. Sasha was on the verge of completing her MA in developmental psychology. Her recent decision to postpone getting her doctorate meant she could work with Max on a more regular basis. The chair of her department at the University of Nevada was disappointed. They lamented the fact that graduate funding had dried up. He blamed the economic downturn. She blamed the Republicans and told him she'd continue when she saved enough money to cover the cost of another degree.

What she didn't tell her professors was that Max taught her more than they did. She didn't need a PhD to know that the theoretical foundations of psychology were way too drug-oriented, not to mention diagnostically slaphappy. No wonder everybody was allegedly so sick these days. In practice, they were pretty much the same as they'd always been, anxious or depressed one minute, happy enough the next. It's just that the spectrum of acceptable emotions was shrinking in direct proportion to the number of prescriptions being filled at Walmart. The fact that pharmacies were located in supermarkets was symptomatic of the real problem. Pills were like food now.

Judging from the expression on Rose's face, Sasha needed to tread lightly. She had that wounded mother look. Sometimes fathers wore this expression, but more often mothers, who seemed to take autism personally. Even if parents didn't blame themselves for their child's condition in the first place, they felt responsible for anything less than a full recovery. Out of guilt, they often pressured their kids too much. Like stage mothers. Or like fathers coaching their sons' football teams as though recovery were a touchdown and normalcy the two-point conversion.

"Don't be silly," Rose said. "Hopes can never be too high."

"I guess it depends on the context. In this case, expecting too much is unfair."

"Expecting too little is even more unfair."

"I've seen it work both ways."

Sasha appreciated the value of wishful thinking as a coping mechanism. It certainly beat wallowing in despair. But Rose's blind optimism seemed selfish, if not outright intolerant, a refusal to accept Max's fundamental right to be Max. He was a person, after all, not just a set of symptoms. Autonomous as well as autistic. Sasha wanted to say that sometimes kids just need to be loved for who they are, regardless of who we want them to be. No doubt it would have sounded like an insult.

"It's Max's recovery, not ours." Sasha checked her watch. Recess was over. "We've got to let him set the pace. Two steps forward and one step back."

Rose was appalled. Without realizing it, she had a recovery timetable ticking in the back of her mind. Max would be cured in time for first grade. From her perspective, he was progressing at a spectacular rate, far in excess of *ten tries, six of them successful without assistance*, which sounded suspiciously like Dr. Dillard's initial prognosis. *Your son may never advance beyond the mental age of five or six.* Two steps forward and one step back just wasn't good enough.

"I'll be in the study if you need anything," Rose said.

More often than not, mothers said something to this effect when they left therapists alone with their children. Sasha understood it as a veiled assertion of control, a reminder that she was in the Barrons' house working with their child on their dime, thank you very much. Who could blame them for being territorial in the face of such a profound invasion of privacy? It wasn't easy, leaving your son in the hands of an almost total stranger, whose intervention often seemed to intensify rather than ameliorate his temper tantrums. Resistance was part and parcel of the therapeutic process, by patients and parents alike. Even under the circumstances, Rose sounded more like an Avon lady than an incensed mother, yet another symptom of denial. Sasha preferred Max's more straightforward expression of displeasure, fists and all.

* * *

Nothing felt real anymore. Waging virtual war was taking its toll on Todd's judgment, maybe even his integrity. Colonel Trumble summoned him to report on the civilian casualty episode. Their meeting was really just a formality, part of the protocol of due diligence designed to justify drone warfare. The fact that they called it an episode rather than a massacre did nothing to alter the outcome. Two children and one mother dead. The father, who may or may not have been an insurgent, wasn't even at home. There were plenty of judgment calls leading up to the control glitch cited in the official report. Todd could have recommended an investigation. He didn't.

Colonel Trumble's office was in the 432nd Air Expeditionary Wing complex overlooking Creech's manned aircraft runways. Todd liked spending time in this part of the base, where actual planes were flown by actual pilots. He had met with the colonel several times before to discuss the possibility of rotating drone pilots in and out of combat duty. They agreed it was a good idea, but it wasn't cost effective. Once pilots cycled into drone squadrons for two or three years, the cost of requalifying them to fly F-15 Eagles was prohibitive. The ideological mandate for flying drones instead of manned planes was that they saved lives. The pragmatic bottom line was that they saved boatloads of money, particularly on the training end of things. The air force was on the verge of allowing enlisted recruits to train as drone operators, a policy the army and marines had long since implemented. Why train officers when you can recruit joystick jockeys for next to nothing? Even Todd had to admit they handled drones as well and sometimes better than traditional pilots. But without combat experience, they lacked the martial ethics that transform killers into warriors.

The colonel hated serving Stateside as much as Todd did. He'd fought two tours in Iraq, two in Afghanistan, and was eager to volunteer for his fifth when his leg got blown off by an IED. He called it the dog shit incident by way of setting up his favorite punch line. "I really stepped in it that time, didn't I?" Calling it an incident didn't alter the fact that he'd lost his leg. But transforming misfortunes into comedy routines did wonders for his morale. He had an amazing prosthetic device and an even more amazing physical therapy regimen. He walked like any other guy on the base, only straighter, with more determination.

Colonel Trumble always seemed glad to see Todd. He waived off his salute and motioned to a chair. Todd was wary of the informality. Underneath all his horsing around, the colonel was a shrewd officer.

"Coffee?"

"No thanks."

"Bourbon?"

Todd mustered up a snicker, even though it felt inappropriate under the circumstances. Everyone laughed at the colonel's jokes. He was the highest ranking officer on the base.

"How are things out at the trailer park?"

"They've been better."

"So I heard. How's Brown?"

"A little shaky. But he'll be fine."

"Let him fly surveillance for a week or two. Till he gets his mojo back."

"Sounds like a good plan."

"He should be commended for following orders."

"Yes, Sir."

In all good conscience, Todd knew he'd have to delegate this particular assignment. It was one thing to let Brown off the hook, quite another to exonerate him. Captain Frick, his immediate subordinate, would have to do the honors. Since the decision to launch drone strikes was always collaborative, nobody could be held accountable. Untold numbers of combatants and consultants had weighed in on the decision to mount the strike—the CIA, Central Command, Special Ops, a team of data processing contractors, and the lieutenant in charge of boots on the ground. Colonel Trumble was only interested in the chain of command culminating in the strike. As long as the chain was intact, the glitch was a glitch, not a systems failure. He was perfectly satisfied with the official report. It coincided with official policy.

Todd was a military man to the core of his being. As Rose put it, not without a hint of pride, he had been born under the star of order and discipline. But following orders issued on a computer screen felt an awful lot like obeying a machine. He knew what the colonel would say.

"This is the new air force, Major Barron. Get used to it."

That was precisely what he was afraid of. Getting used to it.

He started searching for ways to bring the reality of war closer to home. To be a good fighter pilot, you had to be afraid. You had to risk your life so you wouldn't underestimate the gravity of death. Otherwise war degenerated into cold-blooded killing. Danger was the only real way to recover the visceral threat of combat. First he tried skydiving. The pull of gravity was about as real as you could get. He postponed pulling the cord, prolonging the sensation of falling to maximize the fear factor. But skydiving in Nevada was a far cry from parachuting in Afghanistan. The absence of enemy combatants made it feel like just another day at the office.

News of a fatal accident at Red Rock Canyon convinced him to take up hang gliding instead. The aerial design of gliders was far more temperamental than parachutes. The prone flight position fostered the illusion that there was nothing between you and the unforgiving earth hundreds, even thousands of feet below. Variable wind patterns created black holes that swallowed up even experienced hang gliders.

Unfortunately, Todd was beyond experienced. Wind tunnels posed as much of a threat to air force pilots as five o'clock traffic to race car drivers.

Automatic activation devices. Dive recovery mechanisms. Helmets required by law. Civilian sports were too prophylactic. There was far too much vinyl and canvas involved, protecting you from plunging headlong into danger. Flirting with death wasn't enough. He needed to have a full-blown affair. This was easier said than done. The matrix of simulation and safety was ubiquitous, shielding him from the real deal. He finally resorted to rock climbing without ropes.

*　*　*

It was like autism boot camp in the Barron household. Rose squeezed Floortime therapy into the few hours left before and after Max's ABA sessions with Sasha. No matter how lackluster his response, she managed to rev herself up to dizzying heights of animation. Her voice, which was ordinarily on the sultry side, was elevated at least an octave, resembling a cartoon character on speed. She talked a mile a minute, punctuating everything with exaggerated gestures. Given Max's hypersensitivity, this frenetic approach seemed counterintuitive, like giving Adderall and other stimulants to kids with attention deficit disorder. But even Todd had to admit that the results were remarkable. Max's attention span, which had been virtually nonexistent, improved dramatically. He even started pointing at things, the first step toward learning to talk. Rose operated on the assumption that he understood every last word she said.

"Where's your soldier, Max?"

Rose held out her hands, clenched tight in the manner of guessing games. Max spotted a telltale bazooka peeking through her fingers. He grabbed it and Rose exploded into applause.

"Wowee! You found your soldier! Let's try again."

Rose took another toy soldier from a regiment jumbled in the box by her side. This one carried a machine gun. She knew better than to ask Max to relinquish Bazooka Joe, which was clutched tightly against his chest. Periodically, she had to find a different set of props for their Floortime exercises. After a week or two, Max developed an attachment to the objects. She could no longer touch them without catapulting him into territorial tantrums. The soldiers were Todd's idea. They had been his as a boy. Watching Max play with them provided the kind of connection he craved with his son, oblique but better than nothing.

Rose dangled the second soldier in the air. Max was still fixated on the one in his hand. He started flicking the bazooka with his index finger. Rose let out a loud whoop to attract his attention. She waited until his eyes focused and then made her soldier dance back and forth, just out of reach. Max seemed to smile, possibly even at his mother. When she hid the soldier behind her back, he squealed with what sounded more like delight than autistic screeching. They were actually communicating. In his excitement, Max dropped his soldier. He climbed to his knees and lost his balance. When he recovered, he extended both arms, almost touching his mother's crossed legs. Then he seemed to forget what he was trying to find.

"Where's your soldier now?" Rose shrieked.

She twirled around, revealing the toy behind her back. Max lunged at it and fell giggling to the floor. His eyes were fixed on the ceiling. Rose couldn't tell whether he was having fun or withdrawing into what Todd called Giddy Land, a private place where laughter was hysterical rather than happy. She put the soldier's foot in her mouth, hoping to coax Max into making eye contact. Ordinarily he avoided looking at people's faces. They conveyed too much emotional information, especially his mother's solicitous expression, which threatened to swallow him. Her smile was like a beast baring its teeth. He peered at her out of the corner of one eye, just enough to pinpoint the location of the soldier. He managed to grab it without touching anything warm or soft or wet. It had been a close call. Too close.

Max retreated across the living room toward a blinding light. Rose watched him squinting into the sun, shaking his head like a horse fending off a pesky fly. She rushed over, trying to intervene before it was too late. The window had already hypnotized him, the bright white noise of light eclipsing every other sensation, even his mother's grip on his arm. His eyes alternately squinted and rolled to the side, taking refuge in the partial and the peripheral. He started tiptoeing, first tentatively and then almost frantically, as though struggling to climb out of his body.

If Sasha had been conducting an ABA session, she would have captured Max's attention by any means necessary, hauling him back to the play station if he refused to cooperate on his own. But Rose never forced her son to do anything. Floortime was more about initiating communication than completing tasks. The idea was to inspire Max to desire something so badly he would risk human contact to get it. Enticing him to grab the soldier was secondary to initiating engagement with his mother. The trick was to raise the bar incrementally, moving toward that most elusive and precious of all interactions—eye contact—which made all her hard work worthwhile. She must have progressed too quickly.

The truth was Max hadn't made eye contact with anyone for more than a month. Todd had noticed it. Sasha had made a note of it in her logbook. Rose had ignored this and every other sign that his recovery was stalled, at best. She had even begun withholding information from Sasha, most notably the fact that Max had begun spinning again. This was the first stimming ritual he had outgrown during the course of therapy, the most serious of all with the exception of head-banging. If they left him alone too long, he would spin around the living room until he wobbled and crashed to the floor. Sasha was prone to interpreting even the most incidental setbacks in an outrageously negative light. What she didn't know wouldn't hurt her, especially since Rose had no doubt trampoline therapy would stop the spinning once and for all. Max just needed more proprioceptive input to help integrate the far-flung parts of his body. He was, quite literally, lost in space.

Rose squatted between Max and the window, blocking his view of whatever it was that drew him so compulsively to the light. Optical wavelengths only he could see, perhaps. Or the soothing nothingness of sensory overload. She was afraid he would blind himself. He peered around her, twisting his upper body into a series of impossible positions, like a plant contorting its shape to reach the sun. His motor skills were usually impaired, but he could be extraordinarily agile in pursuit of one of his fetishes. Every time she moved, he moved. They were interacting, to be sure, but the language they were using was too pathological to qualify as actual communication.

"Max! Don't you want to find another soldier?" Rose ran over to the box and grabbed a handful. "These were Daddy's soldiers, did you know that? He used to play with them when he was a little boy. Just like you."

She started lining the soldiers up across the windowsill, something Max himself might do. Arranging objects was apparently much more interesting than playing with them. Rose was wary of feeding into his compulsions. She was desperate. The bright light glinted off their various weapons, yet another enticement. Max remained oblivious to everything but the blanket of light, wrapping his senses in its warm embrace. Rose wished she could draw the drapes, if only to protect his eyes, but Max would go ballistic. She remembered that fateful afternoon when they finally decided to consult with Dr. Dillard about why a boy would spend all day every day glued to a window, staring into the sun.

Max started pulling on his eyelids, another behavior they thought he'd abandoned long ago. Rose refused to believe he was regressing. He had the benefit of the best of all possible treatment options. But there was nothing wrong with looking for yet another program to complement ABA and Floortime. There might be some aspect of his cognitive development she had overlooked. Her Facebook friends had already recommended every weapon in their therapeutic arsenals. So she'd have to strike out on her own. Somewhere in the vast outer regions of the World Wide Web, there must be something truly miraculous, the ultimate cure of cures everyone else had overlooked.

* * *

He likes to stand with his forehead almost touching the glass, drinking in the light. The brighter it is, the more it soothes him. If he concentrates hard enough on the white light, he can't see the streamers things make when they move too fast. Silver and gold with fiery red tails. He can't smell Mommy's perfume, which follows him everywhere. He can't hear his sister popping her gum. He can't even hear the furnace clicking on and off, on and off at maliciously irregular intervals. The light blocks out everything else, bathing his senses in whiteness.

* * *

The civilian casualty episode didn't exactly trigger a conversion experience. Brown was still a beer-guzzling slacker. But he stopped hotdogging and started really listening to Todd's pep talks about the ethics of combat. He deferred to his commander's judgment and tried to act prudently under pressure. The other members of the peanut gallery, most notably Kucher and Poindexter, were not impressed. They razzed him about being teacher's pet in an effort to shame him back into their ranks. Brown dug deep and stood his ground, retaliating the way self-respecting military men have retaliated for millennia. He told them to fuck off.

Recruitment posters list integrity, service, and valor as air force core principles. Once you actually wore the uniform long enough to scuff your boots, you learned that prudence was the better part of valor. Hurling yourself headlong into battle was a heroic fantasy only civilians could afford to entertain. In actual combat you ended up dead, not decorated with medals of honor. In virtual combat, the fact that it was impossible to be killed or even wounded increased the threat of making fatal mistakes. The safer you were, the more likely you were to end up with innocent blood on your hands. It was all the more important to be prudent when your life wasn't on the line.

Paradoxes always abounded in war. They were waged to keep the peace. Hiroshima saved lives. That kind of thing. Drone warfare was especially paradoxical. Virtual pilots thousands of miles away from the action were trigger-happy. Statistically, they were up to two times more likely to bomb mistaken targets. The cause of this itchy trigger finger syndrome had yet to be determined. The psychology of virtual warfare was still in its infancy. It could have been as simple as boredom, not to mention complacency stemming from watching too many video-game deaths on too many computer screens, none of which produced a single drop of blood. The cause could have been physiological rather than psychological, phantom reflexes or synapses firing in response to sense memories registered during countless years of playing war games on laptops. Danger had a way of honing reflexes and tempering the kind of bravado that backfired in real combat. All these factors finally convinced Todd to invite Brown to go rock climbing.

Something about this particular kid spoke to Todd. Brown didn't remind him of himself. Todd was a model of military precision and discipline. Brown couldn't even keep his shirt tucked in. But as clueless as he was when he showed up at Creech, he emerged as the one lieutenant with a hint of the right stuff. In another era, combat missions would have scared the shit out of him. He would have emerged a better man. This new breed of warrior was at a distinct disadvantage. There was virtually no way to instill fear into the exercise of dragging a mouse across a virtual battlefield. Todd knew he was taking a chance, letting Brown into the inner sanctum of his death-defying rituals. There'd be hell to pay if the colonel found out a commissioned officer was climbing without ropes. The air force had invested too much money in his training to play games with death. But they'd left him no choice. The absence of clear and present danger was jeopardizing the integrity of his men. Unless you put skin in the game it was just a game.

Brown had done a little rock climbing growing up near the Shawangunk range in upstate New York. He had preferred getting drunk and chasing tail. But there were several early adolescent years when he and his buddies had to settle for more wholesome pursuits. He was long and lanky and considerably more powerful than Todd. What he lacked in finesse he made up for in brute strength. The first few times out, they used ropes. Todd gave him a few pointers, surreptitiously gauging his willingness to take risks. Brown was a quick study. His technique improved with every climb, magnifying his natural athleticism. He seemed to scale cliffs in a single bound. Todd was more compact and deliberate. It took him two or three moves to accomplish what Brown did in one. Risk was his middle name.

The first time Todd climbed freestyle, Brown just unfastened his gear and started up after him. Zero fanfare. They looked like David and Goliath ascending an almost sheer rock face, becoming one with it. When they reached the top and stood looking over the precipice, Todd debated breaking their pact of silence. He hesitated to put what they were doing into words for fear of killing it. But he didn't want Brown to think they were just being daredevils for the macho thrill of it all. Quite the opposite. If humility wasn't what they were after, it was something close to it. Fighter pilots couldn't afford to be flat out humbled by death. But they needed to have a healthy respect for it, to make sure they were meting it out honorably, not randomly, only when duty demanded the ultimate sacrifice.

"You know why we're doing this, right?"

"Climbing?"

"Without ropes."

"It's more exciting."

"It's more dangerous."

"Bring it on."

Had Brown been a soldier in the field this would have been a classic response. Valor in the face of an imminent enemy threat. But they were thousands of miles away from the nearest combat zone. Something had been lost in translation.

"Bring what on?" Todd asked.

"Danger."

"Danger for the sake of danger?"

"Whatever."

Todd kicked a stone over the cliff. They could barely hear the sound of its impact far below.

"What would you say if I asked you if flying drones is dangerous?"

"I would have said no until a few weeks ago."

"Then what happened?"

"You know what happened."

"All of a sudden it was real, right? Not just another frigging video game."

Brown remained silent for a long time. Vultures were circling at eye level, surveying the deep canyon.

"I guess I learned that the hard way."

"That's why we're here. To keep it real."

A flock of grackles dive-bombed the vultures. Whether they did it to defend their territory, or just for sport, was impossible to determine.

* * *

Rose was surfing the net, trying to track down additional treatment options for Max, when she stumbled across the Source. She googled the neurological and environmental causes of autism for the millionth time, hoping to discover something new. The one thing she learned from Dr. Dillard was that diagnosing the root cause of a medical problem was the first step toward discovering its cure. Then, out of the blue, the Internet manifested testimonials describing autism as a source of enlightenment. At first she thought she had clicked the wrong link. Then she knew that it was meant to be.

> *I was devastated when my son was diagnosed with autism. It felt like a death sentence. My husband had to take a second job to cover treatment expenses, which put a terrible strain on our marriage. We tried everything, to no avail. Our little boy Tony seemed lost to us, locked in his own alien world. Then I found the Source. The power of positive thinking changed everything instantaneously and forever! I came to understand that Tony is differently abled, not disabled. He is perfect and complete in his own special ways. Since that fateful day, Tony has become a source of inspiration. I call him my little prophet. His autism is a blessing in disguise, now that I've learned to listen with more than just my ears.*

> *Kitty Gurnsey*
> *Little Rock, Arkansas*

For a split second, even Rose thought there was something fishy about Kitty's conversion experience. She knew what Todd would say. The power of positive thinking sounded an awful lot like wishful thinking. Then she remembered all the times Max heard and saw things she couldn't hear and see. He had been diagnosed with hypersensitivity, as though the acuity of his five senses were a problem rather than a gift.

At times his otherworldly expressions seemed visionary. Rose was reminded of Hans Asperger's observation that a dash of autism is an essential aspect of genius. What if Mozart and Wittgenstein had been pathologized rather than patronized?

Rose clicked on the link, and the Source changed everything instantaneously and forever, just like Kitty Gurnsey said it would. Its home page was dazzling. Ancient origins notwithstanding, enlightenment was surprisingly user-friendly in the digital age. A soaring orchestral score serenaded a sublime seascape with waves carrying words of wisdom on their crests. As each successive wave broke on the shoreline, the words sank into the sand, making way for new revelations.

> *The source of all knowledge and power is within,*
> *waiting to be summoned at will.*

> *The power of thought is limitless.*

> *Everyone is in complete control of everything.*

An Introductory Guide to All Knowledge and Power started scrolling across the screen, assuring Rose that there were no accidents in the cosmos. At the same time, nothing was predetermined. Rose herself had manifested the answer to all of her questions. She was exactly where she was meant to be, at the Source of the Universe.

Before she even had a chance to finish reading, a voice intervened. The Introductory Guide began to fade, ultimately vanishing altogether. The voice introduced itself as Tashi, one in an eternal series of messengers translating what imposters called the Secret, as though power and prosperity were somehow elusive rather than omnipresent.

> *Think of me not as your guide but as a fellow*
> *sojourner on the path to truth.*

> *Close your eyes and listen to the voice within:*
> *The Source.*

Rose closed her eyes. A chorus of panpipes floated over the voice. Their hollow timbre amplified the rich fullness of Tashi's intonation of the Seven Principles of the Universe.

★ *Thoughts are the most powerful force in the universe, the author of everything.*
★ *Nothing negative can happen when we think positive thoughts.*
★ *What we resist persists.*
★ *Disease is a state of mind; every illness of the body can be healed by healthy thoughts.*
★ *Lack and scarcity are illusions; the universe is infinitely abundant.*
★ *Gratitude manifests things to be grateful for.*
★ *Perfection, prosperity, and peace are the divine birthright of collective consciousness.*

Open your eyes.

Several icons appeared on the screen, including the eye of Horus, yin-yang, and ⇔, the symbol for the Law of Infinite Return. Rose clicked on ⇔ and the voice started reciting the Seven Principles all over again. It could have been conjugating Latin verbs for all she cared. Tashi's website was a living, breathing thing. The word made flesh. Her voice inhabited the home page the way oracles inhabited Delphi. One click of the mouse and the mysteries of the universe would unfold, one galaxy after another, all of them underscored by what sounded like the harmony of the spheres. Her voice. It was all about Tashi's voice.

A vast network of links was designed to either soothe or inspire, depending on the heart-centered intention of the acolyte. Rose gravitated toward the former in the wake of her discouraging Floortime session with Max. She clicked on the rod of Asclepius, the icon corresponding to the Fourth Principle. *Disease is a state of mind.* A river appeared, winding through a landscape of astounding fecundity. Healing thoughts eddied in its currents. With the help of time-lapse photography, a brilliant sun rose over its placid waters. A list of payment plans rose with it.

For a flat fee, pilgrims could consult their oracle as often as they wished. Celestial membership included enrollment in weekly webinars. For an additional $200 a month, Higher Power members received a pass code authorizing direct contact with Tashi herself via e-mail. The most expensive option, the Cosmic Consciousness Club, granted access to her cell phone number. Less exalted members could purchase telephone time at reasonable rates beginning at $75 per call. No one, not even the CCC, ever met with Tashi in person. Not unlike God, her invisibility enhanced her mystique. Rose clicked on MasterCard and opted for the Introductory Plan, which included a complimentary five-minute phone conversation. Just hearing Tashi's voice would be worth the price of admission: $79.99.

Navigating the website was like taking a virtual tour of the natural wonders of the world. Every trackless beach and desert was backlit by a brilliant sunset. Every towering peak was caressed by rays of light reaching like the hand of God from the firmament. The site's resources were as inexhaustible as truth itself, with more links than the Great Chain of Being. There were links to mantras and meditations and visualization exercises. Links to daily, even hourly aphorisms, hailing from antiquity to the newest of New Age practices. The core beliefs of an amazing array of prophets, mystics, and philosophers of the soul were distilled into pithy slogans you could contemplate on your way to the supermarket or while getting your hair done. Tashi understood that spirituality needed to keep pace with tweets and sound bites, and she tailored her teachings accordingly. The Source was a practice, like naturopathy and yoga, a way to live more mindfully every minute of every day.

The scope of the World Wide Web paled in comparison with the vision of the Source, which encompassed the entire universe. But on that very first day, prior to her unforeseen cosmic conversion, Rose was focused on one little boy trapped in the confines of his own mind. She returned to the main menu and clicked on the rod of Asclepius once again. This time the link ushered her into a world free of disease, where pathology was more a state of mind than an actual affliction.

Visualizing health will manifest well-being.

Illness is, above all, a failure of the imagination.

A preliminary disclaimer acknowledged that genetics and heredity could potentially figure into the etiology of disease. But inherited tendencies were activated by lack of spiritual and cognitive integrity, the ultimate cause of everything from cancer to the common cold. The Source provided a lengthy list of so-called diseases, each with its own link. More often than not, they reflected unresolved emotional issues. Adult-onset diabetes was rooted in self-hatred, often exacerbated by parental or marital rejection. Autoimmune disorders were a physical manifestation of spiritual suicide. Hemorrhoids were a nagging reminder of chronic rage. A second disclaimer dismissed the belief that the power of positive thinking could cure anything and everything, something rival philosophies liked to claim. Truth be told, there was nothing to cure to begin with. Disease models of medicine predisposed patients to manifest symptoms. Diagnoses were like magnets, attracting rather than preventing illness.

Rose was conflicted. In spite of Dr. Dillard's woeful negativity, his diagnosis had provided a kind of relief. It gave her something to fight against, an adversary she could overwhelm with the help of modern medicine. A part of her believed that setting up Max's treatment guaranteed a cure. The more elaborate the treatment, the more quickly he would progress toward normalcy. But dozens of tests and procedures and hundreds of therapy sessions later, Max was pretty much where he started, smack in the middle of the spectrum. She couldn't bear the thought of another nine months of the same, especially when adjusting her thoughts promised to change things instantaneously and forever. At the very least, the Source promised to transform desperation into hope. She clicked on Autism, fully expecting the miracle that had eluded her thus far.

> *Autism consists of superficial neurological impairment on the one hand and profoundly enhanced powers of intuition and cognition on the other.*

> *This spectrum of abilities proves that children on the spectrum are genetically predisposed to both autism and spirituality.*

> *By spirituality we mean heightened cognitive capacities, as follows:*

> *Contemporary culture overemphasizes left-brain functions, thereby undermining capacities related to the right brain, including intuition, spontaneity, creativity, and varieties of spiritual experience valued more highly in ancient and Eastern realms less infatuated with the cult of reason.*

> *Spirituality and transcendence are only possible when we strike a balance between right- and left-brain functioning, connecting the two hemispheres through heightened neural activity.*

> *Our souls are hungry for this balance.*

> *Children with autism choose to tolerate heightened brain activity in order to elevate humanity to higher levels of spiritual expression.*

> *The value of a spiritual view of autism is that it transforms limitation and helplessness into a sense of purpose and meaning.*

We should be listening to the voice of autism rather than silencing it.

Autism is prophetic.

Rose had never thought much about spirituality. When they were first married, she and Todd had gone to church a few times, mostly for show. His first commanding officer was a born-again Christian. But even the prospect of promotion paled in comparison with Sunday mornings in bed. The body was infinitely more important than the soul, especially in those early days before the kids were born. In retrospect, her spiritual indifference corroborated the idea that flesh and spirit had, in fact, been sundered by the same misguided cultural forces that pathologized her son. No one, least of all doctors and ministers, ever considered the possibility that we might be naturally healthy and intrinsically whole. The doctrine of genetic predisposition was no different than the theory of original sin. The focus was always on what was wrong rather than what was right.

An overwhelming sense of relief washed over what must have been Rose's soul. Without realizing it, she had blamed herself for her son's condition. She was too protective a mother to do otherwise. Never mind the fact that Maureen was a perfectly normal kid. Her success with her daughter was more an accusation than a comfort, further evidence of her failure with Max. Within minutes, the Source assuaged her guilt. The website employed a kind of logical inevitability that appealed to Rose's rational side, paving the way, step by step, for insights she had never thought possible. She, of all people, had been trapped in a web of negativity, treating autism as though it were an illness rather than an opportunity. By the time she logged off the site, hours later, she understood that no one was to blame for Max's condition. No one was to blame for anything. Seen from an enlightened perspective, everything was as it should be in the universe.

*   *   *

The best place is Daddy's closet. Everything is orderly. Everything smells the same, like leather, unless he buries his nose in the shirts. They all hang facing the same direction, smelling like laundry detergent. There are three flight suits and one dress uniform with gold buttons that shine even when the door is almost closed. He always leaves it open a crack because Daddy does. Otherwise someone might notice and find him in there.

He isn't hiding. He's protecting himself. In the back, behind a row of sweaters, there's room to sit all curled up in a ball, the way he wishes they'd let him sit at the dinner table. He never gets to do what he wants except in the closet. Or at night when they're all asleep. He wants to be left alone. To be safe.

Belts pose the only real threat. Daddy keeps messing them up, hanging short ones next to long ones. There are five hooks and nine belts. Ten counting the one Daddy wears to work. Sometimes three hang together, crowding one hook and leaving another one empty. Two belts per hook are fine, as long as they're both the same color and the same length. He sorts them out before climbing onto his shelf. Black with black and brown with brown. He gives the widest belt its own hook.

He's taking a chance. Daddy keeps track of things and might notice. But sitting in a closet with belts hanging every which way is unthinkable. No better than the living room or even his bedroom, ever since they dismantled the lock. Someone is always barging in. Something is always out of place. Out of control. He takes comfort where he can find it. Daddy's closet is safe.

~ III ~

Everything was business as usual after the civilian casualty episode. Captain Frick carried out Colonel Trumble's order to commend Brown for following orders. Otherwise, nobody ever mentioned it again. Day in and day out, the most serious threat in the trailer was boredom. The US Air Force had developed an arsenal of amphetamines to fend off battle fatigue. Since Chair Force drone pilots weren't technically on combat duty, they had to rely on caffeine. Todd was the only coffee drinker. According to his calculations, this said a lot about the demographics of the squad. The drug of choice was Mountain Dew. The recycling bin was overflowing with cans by noon, especially on Mondays. Weekend warriors one and all. Presumably their bins at home were just as jammed with beer bottles.

Business as usual meant everybody was in surveillance mode. A flick of a switch could catapult any one of the drones into kill mode. This simple fact convinced bad guys thousands of miles away to lay low for weeks at a time. What the Pentagon called the Panopticon Effect supposedly saved lives and money. A single Predator drone could paralyze an entire region with paranoia, even in North Waziristan. That was the good news. The bad news was that it made war boring as hell. No wonder guys had itchy trigger fingers. Anything to break the monotony.

Every pilot had his own SO, a sensor operator tasked with tracking targets with the drone's million dollar eye in the sky. The sensor was always in motion, rotating and swiveling and zooming its way into the secret recesses of enemy territory. Even though pilots actually pulled the trigger in combat mode, they had to rely on their sidekicks to steer laser-guided bombs home to mama. They worked as a team, surrounded by more than a dozen monitors transmitting electro-optical digital images, radar scans, full-motion video streams, and 3-D terrain mapping. The sheer volume of information at their fingertips was mind-numbing. In the spirit of professional multitaskers, they alleviated the anaesthetizing effects of overstimulation with yet more stimulation, inventing interactive games to play with each other, the more juvenile the better. Their favorite was an unmanned aerial vehicle version of Slug Bug.

"Read 'em and weep, fellas," Brown said. "A bona fide Volkswagen."

"A bug?"

"A Jedi."

"You mean Jetta," said Gomez.

Gomez wasn't really correcting Brown. They were thinking together, as usual. He had actually spotted the VW even before Brown did, smack in the middle of one of their shared screens. But good SOs never stole their pilot's thunder. Batman and Robin. The Lone Ranger and Tonto. Brown and Gomez.

"Jedi. Jetta. Good for a point, one way or the other."

"Hold your horses," Kucher said. The senior member of the squad, he resented the fact that Brown was so cocky. "Sedans don't count."

"It's red."

"Red as a fairy's cherry."

"Big deal."

"Green and red are wild cards."

"Since when?"

"Last week."

"Says who?"

"Ask Franklin."

"Fair ball," said Franklin. "Chalk one up for Brown."

Captain Franklin was the scorekeeper. The rules were so complicated, he used a spreadsheet to tally up points. He also acted as referee when sightings were disputed, almost always by Kucher. Franklin inherited a kind of gravitas from his father, a Seattle judge who still couldn't believe his son had joined the air force. The odds were certainly against it from a socioeconomic point of view. Franklin was the only white collar son in the trailer.

"Who's winning?" Poindexter asked. He knew perfectly well that Brown was in the lead, but he couldn't resist the chance to rub Kucher's face in it. Everyone was sick and tired of hearing the old guy bitch and moan. Almost inconceivably, Kucher was born before Pac-Man was invented, when kids still played foosball. Anyone over thirty was considered obsolete in the digital age.

With the exception of Todd and Captain Frick, who had both trained at the academy, Kucher was the only member of the squad who wished they were flying F-15s and 16s rather than Reapers and Predators. Back in the day, there was reason to believe that exceptional drone operators might eventually qualify for redeployment as traditional combat pilots. A decade later, guys like him were more trouble than they were worth. What the air force really needed was recruits accustomed to spending every waking hour staring at hand-held devices and computer screens. They never pined for actual combat duty because simulation felt more real than the real thing.

"Don't be such a sore loser," Poindexter said.

"Not so fast," Kucher said. "Ring me up. Five big ones."

"An SUV?"

"A jackal."

Half the time, they cruised over regions too remote or too poor to offer much in the way of cars, let alone SUVs. Locals were more apt to ride donkeys or yaks. So they developed an elaborate system of equivalencies. American cars, which were relatively rare in Afghanistan, were worth ten points. So were wild goats and ibex, which had been hunted almost to extinction. Grey wolves and striped hyenas were worth nine points, along with limousines and high-end sports cars. They usually played to 100, which could take either hours or days, depending on flight patterns. There had only been one sighting of the ever elusive Beetle, an automatic game winner. Judging from the ensuing ruckus, Todd thought they'd spotted Osama bin Laden himself barreling down the Karakoram Highway. The entire trailer went bananas.

When they got tired of Slug Bug, they played Scavenger Hunt or Burqa Bingo. The same kind of squabbles broke out, no matter what game they played. They sounded more like kids in backseats than pilots in cockpits. Todd felt like the grumpy dad, always on the verge of telling them to knock it off. But he knew better than to feed into this dynamic. It was a losing battle. Discipline for the sake of discipline, the bread and butter of the old air force, was counterproductive with this new breed of pilots. Every time he intervened, the whole squad lapsed into sullen silence. Besides, they actually performed better when they were horsing around. The camaraderie of troops in the field was sadly lacking among drone pilots, who bunked in bachelor pads rather than with each other. Slug Bug did wonders for their morale.

Lieutenant Farley was the only spoilsport. He was way too focused to indulge in fun and games. At first Todd chalked it up to maturity. Then he realized something wasn't quite right upstairs. Farley's attention span was preternatural. For hours at a time, his eyes never strayed from his monitors. He executed his maneuvers with robotic precision, as though he himself were a drone. It got to the point where Todd actually wished he would start farting around, if only to prove he was still human. There was a point beyond which detachment was a liability rather than an asset. Todd notified Colonel Trumble, requesting a medical evaluation that resulted in a clean bill of health. Given the exigencies of supply and demand, post-traumatic stress diagnoses were increasingly rare, especially for guys like Farley who had never stepped foot on a battlefield. The air force couldn't train officers fast enough to keep up with the proliferation of remotely piloted aircraft deployed in the war on terror.

Todd knew damned good and well that his RPA squad was at least as prone to PTSD as combat pilots, possibly even more so. They worked longer hours, day in and day out, with no better way to blow off steam than playing Slug Bug. They rarely got the chance to pull the trigger, which is why most men joined the armed forces in the first place. Adrenaline rushes were the real drug of choice, not Mountain Dew. Even when they did see action, the aftermath was gruesome rather than heroic. Drone pilots were expected to verify the accuracy of their strikes, flying back and forth until the dust settled to assess the damage. SOs zoomed into ground zero, and pilots filed the reports. Whatever satisfaction they derived from missions accomplished was always tempered by high-resolution pictures of wreckage strewn with body parts, something Todd had never witnessed during his three tours of active duty overseas. This had been Farley's undoing. He liked dropping bombs as well as the next guy. He just didn't have the stomach for what Colonel Trumble euphemistically called the paperwork.

Todd monitored Farley's missions much more closely than anyone else's on the squad. For over a month he had been tasked with surveilling the same compound, which was either a hotel or a terrorist cell or both. He had gotten to know the proprietors, an old couple whose grandchildren visited on weekends. Their routines had become his routines. The old guy snuck cigarettes out behind his work shed. His wife was always prowling around trying to catch him in the act. When she went to bed he smoked brazenly on the porch with their customers, mostly middle-aged men traveling alone, either businessmen or al Qaeda operatives or both.

Todd watched Farley watching everyone's every move in and out of the hotel. He developed a certain fondness for the couple, whose volatility spiced up many a dull day in the trailer. They were always throwing up their hands or storming off in a huff. Todd could tell from their body language that their fights aroused them. An hour later, all was miraculously forgiven. No wonder guys like Farley disappeared down the rabbit hole. It was one thing to bomb total strangers, quite another to waste the familiar faces of an elderly couple still very much in love. Judging from his expression, Farley was oblivious to the domestic drama unfolding on his screens. But the way he white-knuckled his joystick told a different story. He gripped it like a man dangling over a precipice only he could see. Letting go required a grasp of another reality, the actual life he no longer lived outside the trailer.

Farley was the first to arrive every morning and the last to leave. He lingered at his station even after a relief pilot took his place at the controls, still mesmerized by his monitors. The rest of the squad was halfway home by the time he finally wandered out to the parking lot. Nobody carpooled even though they all drove the same arrow-straight highway through the desert. They needed the time alone to decompress. Almost every single day, they commuted thousands of miles from the greater Middle East to Las Vegas, a distance Farley was too traumatized to travel. He was always in either Afghanistan or Pakistan, depending on the mission. And the mission was never ending.

* * *

Rose dragged a lawn chair out into the middle of the yard. She studied the position of the sun, trying to gauge what the Source called the daily equinox. The idea was to sit facing the precise place the solar arc would peak that afternoon, to maximize her receptivity. As with everything, it was reciprocal. The more energy she absorbed, the more she would emit, giving Tashi the cosmic connection she needed to conduct a productive session. Unlike old-fashioned psychics, who relied on face-to-face contact, Tashi had access to the energetic equivalent of Verizon wireless. As long as initiates aligned their solar quadrants, she could hear them loud and clear.

When Rose made the appointment, the website manifested a long list of instructions. A great deal could be accomplished during her complimentary five-minute phone conversation, provided telekinetic channels were wide open. Rose kicked off her sandals and dug her toes into the grass. She took off her sweater to expose her skin to the elements. She started meditating with eyes wide open, orienting outward rather than inward to erase the boundary between herself and the world. The goal was to launch her astral body before she even picked up the phone. Since everything happened for a reason, nothing was left to chance. She waited until the third ring. The number three embodied a union of body, mind, and spirit in the circle of eternity where past, present, and future coalesced in the now.

"Rose Barron?"

"Speaking."

"Please hold."

Rose was deeply disappointed. Though she had only recently discovered the Source, she had been waiting for this moment for what seemed like a lifetime. The prospect of hearing Tashi's voice on the phone had sustained her over the course of a particularly difficult weekend. Maureen had sprained her ankle practicing for cheerleader tryouts. Todd was outraged that grade schools even had cheerleaders, let alone the fact that his daughter thought she was old enough to join the squad. His response was disproportionate, a clear indication that something he wasn't at liberty to discuss was bugging him at work. Then there was Max, who seemed to regress even further on days when his father was home. Every chance she got, Rose slipped into the study to log on to the website. She hadn't realized how desperately she needed refuge, a place where everything wrong was made right by the mere sound of Tashi's voice. The moment of truth had finally arrived, and an automated operator had put her on hold. Panpipes serenaded her as she waited yet another lifetime before the epiphany of Tashi herself.

"Rose?"

"Tashi?"

"I would introduce myself, but I feel like we're already old friends."

"I can barely hear you," Rose said.

Tashi's voice seemed a million miles away. In spite of Rose's efforts to live in the here and now, she almost wished she were back online so she could turn up the volume. The extent to which the Source relied on technology seemed to undermine its spiritual credibility. Then Tashi performed her first miracle.

"Turn ever so slightly toward the sun," Tashi said. "You're off-kilter."

Rose shifted in her chair.

"Not that way. To the left."

Rose moved an inch or two the other way.

"There," Tashi said. "Now we're perfectly aligned."

Her voice came through crystal clear. It seemed to emanate not from Rose's cell phone but from some place deep within. Words scarcely seemed necessary. The timbre of the voice was what mattered, vibrating at a frequency that made Rose listen as she had never listened before, to herself as well as to Tashi. So this was cosmic consciousness, she thought, and the idea traveled like a seismic wave rippling through the oceanic depths of a universal mind.

"Breathe," the voice said.

Rose inhaled into her solar plexus, the way the online yoga tutorial had taught her to breathe. She kept the phone receiver as close as possible to her mouth so Tashi could hear the air passing in and out. Psychics claimed they could read palms and tea leaves, not to mention varicose vein patterns and even moles, especially ones with hairs growing from their roots. Tashi specialized in deciphering the far more eloquent language of what she called cosmic winds, which blew with each breath, cleansing the body of toxins and the soul of secret fears.

"Don't worry," Tashi said.

"About what?"

"About anything. Let go of fear and doubt and regrets."

"I'm trying."

"No need to try. Just relax and breathe."

Tashi breathed with her as precious seconds ticked by. Rose tried not to think of time and space and the $79.99 package deal, including a complimentary five-minute conversation consisting primarily of breathing. There would be hell to pay if Todd found the charge on their monthly statement. Good thing he was too busy at work to find time to pay the bills.

"I understand your concern," Tashi said. "But thinking negative thoughts will manifest negative outcomes."

Had she been thinking negative thoughts? Tashi seemed more aware of what was streaming through Rose's mind than she was. It occurred to her that she seldom paid close attention to the random clutter of ideas between her ears. Rather than harnessing their energy, she stumbled through life almost entirely unconscious of the power of consciousness. She tried to reorient her thoughts, which seemed hopelessly trivial, if not negative. At the very least, she tried to avoid dwelling on the $79.99.

"I can hear him trying to comfort you," the voice said.

"Him?"

"Your son."

"Did you read my profile online?"

"Why bother? Your energy is telling me everything I need to know. Can you feel the current connecting us?"

Rose felt nothing beyond an overwhelming urge to lie about feeling nothing. A lot of good it would do since Tashi would probably intuit the lie anyway. Rose closed her eyes to concentrate and then opened them again. She was supposed to orient herself outward, not inward. She tried harder, focusing her attention on the telepathic vibrations of the voice itself. Then she remembered that this, too, was a mistake. Cosmic connections relied on relinquishing rather than exercising will power. She tried to stop trying altogether, something problem solvers always found counterintuitive. Rather than forcing what couldn't be forced, she needed to let go.

"I'm sorry. I'm fairly new at this—"

"No need to be sorry, Rose. Everything is as it should be in the universe."

"What about Max?"

"Especially Max. That's what he's trying to tell you. Worrying about him is blocking your ability to hear him."

"What's he saying?" Rose asked.

"If you listen carefully, you can hear him too."

Rose listened. She heard the wind in her lungs and in the trees, strumming a distant chime. She heard a car alarm, honking incessantly. A lawn mower, possibly a weed whacker, coughed and sputtered. A siren wailed louder and louder, drowning out everything else until it passed. She blamed the siren for her inability to hear Max. The cacophony of the material world was deafening.

"What do you hear?" Tashi asked.

"Sirens. A car alarm."

"You're stuck on a temporal plane. Max is communicating on a much higher level."

"What do you mean?"

"Your son is a shaman, Rose."

"How do you know?"

"He's speaking a universal language, channeling the energy of our time."

Of course. All the pieces, which had been scattered by Max's diagnosis, fell into place. Prior to discovering the Source, Rose would have been hard-pressed to define the word *shaman*, let alone apply it to her very own son. Over the past week, she had learned dozens of words that completely altered the way she interpreted the world. *Monism. Mandala. Chakra. Bodhisattva.* In retrospect, the paucity of her spiritual vocabulary was shocking. She scarcely had language to describe the transcendental beauty of the natural world, let alone Max's transcendent nature. His diagnosis was equally impoverished. *Autism.* The word was intrinsically pathological, a self-fulfilling prophecy that hindered rather than helped her son express his full potential.

"You mean he's gifted, not sick."

"Seers are often misunderstood."

"I knew it!" Rose said.

"Of course you did. You're his mother."

Rose started crying for the first time since Max's diagnosis. She hadn't dared to let her guard down before, for fear of falling apart. Now she felt protected enough to acknowledge the tremendous burden she felt as the parent of a child with autism. Medical science had stopped blaming mothers exclusively, but the history of the disease still referenced Bettelheim's infamous refrigerator theory. Starved for attention by frigid mothers, children withdrew in self-defense. It didn't help that Max was more sensitive to her touch than anyone else's, as though maternal intimacy were threatening rather than comforting. His claustrophobia made sense now. He was more, not less, in touch with her. He was more in tune rather than out of touch with the world.

"Everyone will try to cure him," Tashi continued. "You must fight with all your strength as a mother to make sure he is never cured of his visions. Facilitate rather than censor them. Learn to speak his language so he feels free to speak ours. Unless someone else intuits the message, it will be lost. And so will he."

"How can I help him?"

"It's the other way around, Rose. Max can help you."

"Not if I can't hear what he's saying."

"Listen again. What do you hear?"

"Another ambulance. There's too much going on. I can't hear a thing."

"You're hearing what he's channeling. The message itself."

"What does it mean?"

"You said it yourself, Rose. There's way too much going on way too fast. Too much noise. Too many toxins. Too many screens bombarding us with too many images. X-rays, radio waves, microwaves. Waves of anxiety masked with too many pills and potions. Max is manifesting how we all feel deep down, alternately overstimulated and numb in self-defense."

"I thought you said he wasn't sick."

"He isn't. Illness is an illusion."

"Then why is he in so much distress?"

"Because he feels like no one is listening to him."

"It's not fair. He's just a little boy."

"The universe never gives us more than we can handle, Rose. The fact that Max was chosen to carry the message led you to the Source, didn't it? This is the first step of a journey that will teach you both to live without being distracted by all that white noise. Max is your guide. Once his message has been fully integrated into your spiritual practice, his mission will be complete. He will be free to live a normal life."

A bell started tolling in the distance. At first Rose thought the sound came from the Catholic church down the block. Then she realized the bell was signaling the end of their consultation. Five minutes had utterly changed the way she experienced the world. Imagine what ten minutes could accomplish! She cradled her cell phone in both hands, trying to hold on to their connection as the chimes receded into cyberspace, carrying Tashi's voice along with them. Even before they signed off, Rose felt abandoned. Bereft. Tashi must have sensed her distress.

"Don't worry, Rose. I'm not going anywhere. The Source is always with you. Just listen."

In the abstract, Rose felt certain this was true. But she couldn't wait to call again, to hear Tashi talking directly to her. There was something clarifying about the voice itself. Like chanting, the medium was the message, a soothing, healing wedding of mind and spirit. Rose had already exhausted the perks of her introductory package. Additional calls would cost $75, a paltry sum in comparison with the wealth of knowledge Tashi had to offer. If Todd noticed the charges on their credit card, she'd just tell him the truth. The Source was an integral part of Max's treatment, quite possibly the key to his recovery.

* * *

The living room works best. But it's out there. His bedroom is smaller. In here nobody interrupts him. Nobody tells him to stop or he'll hurt himself. It hurts when they stop him.

He never hurts himself. Even when he falls and hits his head. He's too dizzy to feel anything. In his bedroom he can't get dizzy enough. He can't go fast enough long enough. It's too small. He keeps smashing into things.

He waits until Daddy goes to work. The living room works best when Mommy is on her cell phone. Nobody interrupts him. He spins, his arms spread wide, his head thrown back, until everything goes blank. Blankness blankets him.

* * *

Every Monday morning, what Sasha called the principal players met to discuss Max's progress. She used this term to reinforce the idea that Rose and Todd were equal partners in managing his treatment. For the first few months, Sasha did most of the talking. Even though she was considerably younger, they deferred to her professional authority. She tried to assure them that Max would respond as well, if not better, to their therapeutic interventions. Autism didn't alter the fact that he was their son. Todd in particular was skeptical. Max seemed to shrink from his parents most of all, as though family members were more menacing than any other human threat, an intimate invasion of the territory he defended with the ferocity of a wounded animal.

Maureen usually sat in on the first few minutes of their weekly meetings. She alone seemed oblivious to the tragedy that had befallen the family. The fact that she accepted Max's behavior at face value was instructive. Parents tended to blame themselves for things kids took for granted. As far as Maureen was concerned, Max was first and foremost an annoying little brother. Guilt never compelled her to overdetermine the cause or effects of his condition, which she routinely used to advantage. The fact that Max demanded so much attention left Maureen free to do her own thing. When she wanted to pull focus, she just flaunted her normalcy. No matter what she did, she was, by default, the good child. In classic firstborn fashion, she was fond of her brother to the extent that he confirmed her position at the top of the pecking order.

The principal players convened around the kitchen table. Informality helped foster the idea that there was nothing extraordinary about discussing the frequency of Max's violent outbursts, or the duration of his catatonic regressions. It was just another Monday morning in the Barron household. Max was still in bed, avoiding the rigors of therapy for as long as possible. On weekends, when Sasha wasn't around, he was the first one up. He liked to watch the early morning sunlight advance across the living room floor, a drama that engaged his attention for hours. But he knew that Sasha was more likely to find him there. Gone were the days when he used to wander into the playroom on his own. The minute her car drove up, he disappeared down the rabbit hole in his bedroom. It took them up to an hour to coax him out.

Todd and Maureen ate breakfast while they talked. The school bus stopped on the corner at 8:10, and Todd had to be on the road by 8:20 to get to work on time. Sasha always asked how the family had fared in her absence over the weekend. As time went on, their responses differed drastically, revealing more about themselves than Max. Strictly speaking, Sasha was a behavioral therapist, not a family counselor. But her training had included several classes on domestic dynamics, which could jeopardize Max's recovery. Children on the spectrum elicited a spectrum of reactions from parents working through their own psychological baggage. If she could discover the cause of their tangled web of emotions, she might begin to unravel it.

"Pass the milk," Maureen said.

"Please," Rose said.

"I'm talking to Daddy."

"Do what you're told."

"Please."

Todd grabbed the milk carton. When he handed it to Maureen, he didn't let go right away. They played a little game of tug-of-war, Todd with a straight face and Maureen giggling until Rose broke it up.

"You're worse than the kids," Rose said, mostly for Sasha's benefit. She actually liked it when Todd horsed around with Maureen. It verified her conviction that they were one big happy family.

Sasha checked her watch. Todd would be leaving shortly, and he had volunteered next to nothing to the discussion. Even Rose seemed less forthcoming than usual, as though she might be hiding something. Sasha's only recourse was to question Maureen, the loose cannon of the family. Secrets didn't stand a chance when she was around.

"Did you play that game we talked about?" Sasha asked.

"What game?"

"Copycat."

"Max was too busy."

"Doing what?'

"Spinning around the living room."

Rose's chair almost tipped over backward as she jumped to her feet. "Get a move on, young lady. You'll miss your bus."

"I haven't finished my cereal."

"Then you'd better start getting up earlier so you'll have more time to eat."

Sasha glanced at her watch again. 8:01. Maureen obviously had time to finish breakfast, but something in Rose's tone of voice convinced everyone at the table to pretend she was late.

"Go get your pack," Rose said. "I'll give you a granola bar for the road."

When Maureen was safely dispatched, Rose sat down again. Todd had spent the intervening time avoiding eye contact. Sasha understood that it was inappropriate to press the point while Maureen was still within earshot. Once the adults were left alone, there was no reason they couldn't discuss her revelation like adults.

"Max is spinning again?" Sasha asked.

Rose wiped crumbs off of her placemat. Todd nodded.

"How much?"

"Once or twice," Rose said.

"A lot," Todd said.

Rose gave him a sharp look. Todd countered with the blandest of bland expressions, which clearly pissed her off. They were one of those couples who didn't need language to communicate. It wasn't just a question of having been married long enough to read each other's minds. Words paled in comparison with their vivid private vocabulary. There was something energetic, even volatile, about their relationship, which seemed to evoke a fabulous sex life. Sasha didn't speculate about such things out of prurience. She was simply gauging the strength of their marriage, to determine whether it could withstand the strain of autism.

"When did it start?" Sasha asked.

"A couple of weeks ago."

"Can you think of any triggers?"

Predictably, Todd sat back and waited for Rose to fill in the blanks. Having provided his customary reality check, he felt his job was finished. Sasha kept looking at Todd even though he, in turn, was looking expectantly at his wife. She was trying to employ body language to encourage him to fill in his own damned blanks. Rose was becoming an increasingly unreliable witness. Her face had resumed the sunny expression she used to mask her fear that Max might not get better. Todd's candor didn't necessarily mean he was less afraid. He was just playing bad cop to his wife's good cop. Somebody had to do it. Couples often vacillated between the two roles, but not the Barrons. Rose was constitutionally incapable of anything short of unequivocal optimism.

"Any change in his routine?" Sasha asked.

Todd helped himself to a hard-boiled egg. Rose watched him peel it. He salted and peppered it. An uncomfortable silence descended on the table, punctuated by the sound of chewing.

"He's been more agitated the last week or two," Sasha said. She flipped through the pages of her logbook. "I noticed a distinct difference ten days ago, to be exact. Any idea why?"

"Beats me," Todd said.

"Rose?"

"Nothing comes to mind."

"He's probably just exhausted," Todd said. "God knows I am. I get crabby and Max spins. Not very scientific, but there you have it."

"More exhausted than usual?"

"Hard to believe, isn't it? That crescent moon thing seems counterproductive. It takes him even longer to fall asleep."

Rose had discovered the crescent moon position online. The idea was to offset Max's tendency to arch his back when he slept, a position that reinforced the disorganization of his nervous system. Todd thought it was so much hocus-pocus.

Sasha was far less skeptical. Spooning with Max—squeezing and pressing him into a C-shape—might help him figure out where he was situated in space, diminishing his anxiety in the crucial minutes before sleep. There wasn't any clinical evidence of the efficacy of this technique. But this was typical of treatments for autism, a fairly recent epidemic with more anecdotal than scientific information at hand.

"That's one way to look at it, Mr. Doom and Gloom." Todd's skepticism finally compelled Rose to chime in. "But he slept through the night several times last week. I'd say the crescent moon is a great success, among other things."

"Can you be more specific?" Sasha asked. She picked up her pen to take notes.

"He's starting to dress himself on a regular basis. He's eating with a fork and drinking out of a regular glass, not a sippy cup."

"Significant mechanical improvements," Sasha said. "Any developmental milestones?"

"He's learning to listen better. Sometimes it looks like he's mouthing words, copycatting what I'm saying. Like the game, only much more sophisticated."

"I've noticed that, too."

"Then why are you two focusing so much on a couple of isolated spinning episodes?" It was more an accusation than a question. "Everybody slips into old patterns once in a while. Overall, Max is making incredible progress."

A red flag went up. Rose's tendency to lump Todd and Sasha together usually signaled an unprecedented level of denial on her part. Sasha wondered if Todd noticed it, too. He pushed his plate back and rested his elbows on the table. He wasn't so much looking at Rose as watching her. Sasha always found his expression difficult to read, the carefully controlled face of an air force officer trained not to betray his emotions. Rose, on the other hand, didn't even need to look at him to know what he thought of her progress report.

"Good point," Sasha said. "It's important not to underestimate Max's progress. At the same time, we need to be realistic."

"See what I mean by doom and gloom? You make reality sound like a limitation."

"Reality is reality," Todd said evenly. "Wishful thinking doesn't change a thing."

He tried not to sound derisive. In turn, Rose tried to ignore how stupid her husband sounded, even more short-sighted, if possible, than Sasha. The Source enabled Rose to transform their myopic perspective into an opportunity for growth. Thoughts were the ultimate reality, far more real than numbers recorded in logbooks.

"There's nothing wrong with visualizing the best possible outcome," Rose said. "It's better than wallowing in negativity."

"Nobody's wallowing in anything."

"What best possible outcome did you have in mind?" Sasha asked.

The question caught Rose off guard. She had obviously overestimated Sasha's capacity to conceptualize Max's complete recovery, let alone manifest it. No doubt her training was to blame, the deficiencies of pure science. Sasha was a behavioral therapist through and through, devoted to positive reinforcement rather than positive thinking.

"Max is a very special child," Rose said. "Quite possibly a prodigy."

Todd and Sasha exchanged glances. A New Age extravagance had crept into Rose's vocabulary, a new level of conviction the bad cop would eventually have to contend with. But for the moment Todd seemed content to let Sasha coax his wife down to earth.

"Sometimes kids just need to be loved for who they are, not who we want them to be." Sasha had been on the brink of this declaration for months. At the risk of insulting Rose, she should have said it long ago. Part of her job was managing expectations, for the sake of parents as well as their children.

"Loving Max for who he is doesn't preclude visualizing who he might become," Rose said.

"I'm wary of visualizing anything with kids on the spectrum," Sasha said. "It's like fanning the fire."

"What do you mean?"

"They visualize way too much as it is. Instead of seeing dust motes swirling in the sun, Max sees solar systems. An alternate universe light years away from ours."

"Isn't there something wonderfully imaginative about that?"

"He's a little boy, not a science fiction writer. He needs to be grounded in the real."

"The real is relative."

"That's a fairly accurate diagnosis of autistic cognition, you know. Believing with every fiber of your being that the real is relative."

"That's obviously not what I meant. I'm just saying we shouldn't underestimate the power of positive thinking."

"If anything, Max's thoughts are too powerful. He can't see beyond them."

"Not just any old thoughts. Healthy thoughts. Thoughts of abundance rather than scarcity."

They weren't exactly in an argument. You can't argue with cheery champions of the best of all possible worlds. Ordinarily Sasha would have let Rose's blind optimism run its course. But something about her investment in perfection seemed to threaten the therapeutic process. It left very little room for Max. They all needed to be on the same page, or at least on the same planet, to facilitate his recovery.

"Trust me," Sasha said. "His world is already way too abundant. He can't take it all in. We need to teach him to focus on one thing at a time."

"I'll leave that to you," Rose said. "You're obviously very good at it."

Rose ostensibly meant it as a compliment, but they both detected something dismissive in her tone. Sasha expected as much. Parents could be just as resistant as their children, sometimes even more so. Rose, on the other hand, was surprised at her own audacity. She had come a long way since accepting Dr. Dillard's diagnosis at face value. *Your son may never advance beyond the mental age of five or six.* She remembered Tashi warning her against treatments that might rob Max of his gifts while curing his so-called deficiencies. She was less and less certain what, if anything, was wrong with him.

Todd felt curiously indifferent, watching them spar over Max's prognosis. It was a familiar feeling, symptomatic of his desk job waging virtual war. Umpteen hours a day he surveilled the lives of others thousands of miles away. Feeling like a spectator in his own home was even worse. At least at work he could drag a mouse and a drone would do his bidding. He could push a button and activate a Hellfire missile. There was a two-second lag time as his directives bounced from satellite to satellite, leapfrogging across cyberspace before activating distant launchers. But the fundamental mechanism of cause and effect was still intact, the prerequisite of being the principal player in his own life. Even remote control pilots retained a modicum of control. At home, nothing he did produced the desired result. Everything was inconsequential. He loved his son, who shrank from him rather than loving him back. He loved his wife, and she retreated further and further into la-la land. His daughter's primary emotional relationships were apparently online, given the amount of time she spent on Facebook. Everyone was missing in action, worlds away from here and now. Little wonder he was so detached.

"Sorry to break up the party," Todd said. "Uncle Sam is beating the war drum."

Every Monday Todd excused himself with a variation on the same joke. Pesky old Uncle Sam was always cutting their

~ 83 ~

meetings short, summoning troops from the far corners of the Mojave Desert. Todd didn't really sound sorry about leaving. Even indifference could be exhausting. He was tired of the prospect of treatment with no end in sight. Tired of Sasha's relentless questions. Tired of his wife's relentless optimism. Tired of feeling helpless. Going to work was a pain in the ass, but it provided a haven for husbands of all stripes, a refuge from all that was uncontrollable on the home front.

* * *

Sasha apparently decided that since Max had learned to hold a fork, he was ready to wield a paintbrush. Todd heard about their first session of art therapy after the fact. Otherwise he might have intervened. Quite frankly, Sasha's unwonted leap of faith surprised him. Usually she was eminently pragmatic, a refuge from his wife's delusions. It felt like his ally was betraying him, siding with Rose over how best to negotiate Max's condition. The worst possible approach was expecting too much of him. Give the poor kid a break.

When he got home from work that night, Todd could hear Max screaming even before he pulled into the driveway. It was hot and the windows were open. God knows what the neighbors thought. He followed the screams into the bathroom. Max was in the tub. The water was an alarming shade of red. Rose was trying to wash what looked like gashes on his arms. Max kept slapping back her hands, as though it hurt even more than usual to be touched.

"What happened?" Todd asked, modulating his voice to avoid escalating the situation.

"Nothing much," Rose said. "How was work?"

"What's going on here?"

"What are you talking about?"

"Did he cut himself?"

Rose looked over her shoulder. Her mascara was running, like she'd been crying.

~ 84 ~

"It's paint, not blood," she said. "You're projecting."

"Don't start with me."

"Must have been a rough day at the office."

She was right, as usual. Her sixth sense never failed her, even though he kept his oath never to divulge the logistics, let alone the consequences, of his drone missions. Blood everywhere. One of the rookie pilots had puked all over his keyboard, which Todd took to be a good sign. Evidence that the kid didn't think he was just playing another video game. At the same time, none of the soldiers on the ground in Afghanistan had lost their cookies. Evidence that they were trained soldiers, not wimpy nerds playing at war in Nevada.

"Paint?"

"Art therapy."

"What next?"

"The last thing we need tonight is your negativity. It's been a long day."

"Tell me about it. Do you want me to take over?"

"I'm already all wet." Rose wiped the back of her hand across her eyes, smearing her mascara even more. "Remind me to wear goggles when I give him a bath."

"Try it without the washcloth. It's too scratchy."

She dropped the cloth, and it disappeared into the red depths of the tub. Max struggled just as frantically when she scrubbed him with her fingers. They assumed he was just resisting human contact, as usual. The possibility that he might be cathected to the painted patterns on his arms escaped them. He was so rarely emotionally invested in anything new. Even Sasha had underestimated the success of their first art therapy session.

She had started by painting her own picture. ABA was big on what they called modeling. Todd called it Robotics 101. There was no denying that rewarding a child for aping mindless tasks produced tangible results. Max could now match squares with squares and stars with stars. Once in a while, he even managed to parrot a few words. Rose was ecstatic. But Todd hated the way his son's voice droned when he repeated after Sasha.

"Say you love Daddy," Sasha said.

"You love Daddy."

Max extended his hand and Sasha placed two M&M's in his palm, a red one and a brown one. He ate them both and Sasha made a mental note, which she later recorded in her logbook. Max was expanding his color palette.

"Not me, Max. You."

"You."

Max's hand shot back out, but Sasha ignored it. He started banging his fist on the table.

"Say I love Daddy."

"I love Daddy."

"Good boy, Max."

This time Sasha gave him four M&M's, one red, two brown, and one green. He peered at them out of the corner of one eye and threw the green one across the room before eating the other three. There was a limit to his willingness to tolerate gratuitous novelties. He drew the line at green. Todd wasn't entirely convinced that disembodied words prompted by the promise of sugar really qualified as language. If so, the meaning was clear. What Max really loved were M&M's.

M&M's were on the verge of being replaced by assorted dried fruits, sugarcoated in deference to Max's sweet tooth. This was Rose's innovation, the flavor of the week. She had devoured yet another pseudoscientific book, this one about pediatric nutrition. The author was making money hand over fist claiming that nutrition was the determining factor, both the cause and cure of autism. Fruit in particular could cure anything. Apples and oranges and peaches would transform Max into Rembrandt.

Since Max's vocabulary was primarily visual, Sasha thought painting might unlock his ability to speak spontane-ously rather than by rote. Shapes were like words. For the most part, they still existed in isolation, completely autonomous, which was the primary symptom of autism. Max liked lines because they were lines. He especially loved circles because they were circles. If he could see that lines and circles could be arranged into faces with actual human features, he could say *I love Daddy* with more conviction. It would be a multistep process, translating shapes into things, things into people, and people into something worth caring about.

First Sasha drew a picture of Max sitting at the table with a paintbrush in his hand. He was sitting upright in his favorite outfit—sweatpants and a tee shirt—with a big sheet of blank paper spread out in front of him. Sasha painted a big red smile on his face. She used color judiciously. Everything else was brown in deference to his comfort zone.

The real Max had thrown his paintbrush across the room. He was sprawled over the back of his chair, gawking at something, probably the window, which was infinitely more interesting than whatever Sasha had to offer. She got up and closed the blinds. She retrieved his paintbrush and slipped it back between his limp fingers. He didn't cry out, as he usually did, when his window disappeared. He was too far away to even register a response.

"Look at this, Max. We're drawing a picture."

Sasha manipulated his limbs, trying to get him to sit at the table like the little boy in her picture. He kept collapsing like a puppet severed from its strings. Sasha moved her chair closer to his so he could see her picture even with his chin resting on his chest. In theory. He gave no indication of seeing anything.

"Look at all these circles and lines, Max. You can draw anything you want with circles and lines."

Next Sasha drew a picture of Rose standing over Max's left shoulder. She was pointing at his picture with apparent enthusiasm. Sasha's little mother and son were nothing more than glorified stick figures. But they were remarkably animated. In college, she had taken a couple of cartooning classes. Her favorite comic strip was *B.C.* Its elemental sensibility made sense to her. Nothing was really very complicated. Just profound. This primal approach was the key to her success as a developmental therapist.

Max's stare was no longer vacant. He had managed to find something infinitely fascinating either on his shirt or under the table. His body was still limp but he was popping his lips the way he did when he was lost in his own world. Sasha lifted his head so he could see her drawing. The popping stopped. When she let go, his chin dropped back onto his chest as though his neck couldn't support the weight of his head. The popping resumed.

"That's your mom, Max," Sasha said. "You and your mom. Now let's draw your dad."

Todd's distinguishing feature was his hair, which was cropped short and the same vivid red as Max's mouth. He was smiling, too, equally enthralled by the little boy's picture of nothing.

"What are you drawing, Max?"

She slid his paintbrush, which had fallen to the floor, back into his left hand. Then she loaded her brush with red and started painting circles on the little boy's blank canvas, one after another until there were three rows of four, a perfect rectangle of circles.

Max didn't look up, but his lips had stopped popping somewhere around row two.

She dipped her brush again and painted a stripe on Max's arm. He didn't lash out the way he usually did when someone tried to touch him. He didn't move at all until she started painting the fourth stripe. Then his eyes alone shifted away from whatever it was they were or were not seeing so he could watch what Sasha was doing. The brush flattened the hairs on his arm. Then they inched back up, glistening with paint. Together they watched it dry. Sasha proceeded to the other arm. Max's eyes shifted almost imperceptibly, tracing the pattern of the work in progress, one stripe after another, until there was another sequence of four.

"Four lines on each arm," Sasha said. "Four circles in each row."

Sasha pointed to each stripe, one after another, and then to each circle on the canvas. Max's eyes followed her every move.

"Next time you'll do it yourself. You'll count to four with your paintbrush."

*   *   *

The car goes too fast. He can count all the mailboxes. But he can't add up all the house numbers going forty miles an hour. The speed limit is thirty. Mommy never slows down unless there's a red octagon or a little red circle hanging so high he can barely see it from the backseat. Car seats are like straightjackets, which aren't really straight. Even Daddy says so.

There's a mall with seventeen stores, a theatre with sixteen screens, three drive-ins, and hundreds of cars parked between diagonal lines. Two with their lights left on. Some parked backward, which is upsetting, so he counts the ones with little balls on their antennas instead.

There's way too much going on way too fast. When things get really bad he rolls his fingers up into a little telescope. He closes one eye and raises the scope to the other, like a captain on a ship. That way he can zoom in on one thing at a time. Everything else disappears. He can still hear what isn't there so he groans to focus the noise inside. Mommy turns on the radio, which is fine as long as no one talks. He changes the pitch of his groan to the same key as the song on the radio.

He likes it better at home where no one can look at him through the window. People in other cars glare at Mommy. She drives too fast. People's faces are terrible. They never stay the same. One minute they smile, even when they have food stuck in their teeth. The next they look like murderers on TV. If he looks through the window they look back.

He focuses his little telescope on the white circle in the blue square. He doesn't like squares and he doesn't like the chair in the circle. But he loves the wheel on the chair. There's another circle on top of a line. Like the little balls on car antennas, only much bigger. Nothing is bigger than the wheel. He's never seen such a big circle, not even at home.

~ IV ~

Todd left work even later than usual, well after the swing shift commander had everything under control. Telltale intelligence had been gathered on his watch, and he wanted to see whether the bombed compound was really a viable target. Undercover operatives picked through the rubble for hours before they were able to collect enough evidence to corroborate the kill. The strike had, in fact, taken out Inayatullah, a Taliban commander. They finally found his left hand, incinerated but still wearing a wedding ring matching the description of the one placed on his finger by his wife, Wasila, who was not a Taliban commander. It turned out she was also killed in the strike. So it goes.

Rose would be pissed when he got home, but that was nothing new. Todd had been missing dinner a lot lately, ostensibly due to an accelerated rate of offensives. Winter was approaching, and terrorists and other beasts hibernated in the high country. Colonel Trumble issued an order to make hay while the sun shines, by which he meant kill as many bastards as possible before the snow flew. Big game hunting season in Nevada primed the pump for manhunts in Pakistan. Brown and Gomez had already bagged their quota of elk and antelope. Thankfully, there were no quotas on men. Bad guys were always in season. They were just easier to track in September than in December.

If Todd had stopped to think why he didn't mind working late, he would have realized hunting season was a lame excuse. He didn't stop to think about it. Ordinarily, he was as introspective as the next guy. But under the circumstances, he couldn't afford to be self-aware. Acknowledging that things were going from bad to worse at home would do more harm than good. Just when he thought he was coming to terms with Max's condition, his wife went off the deep end. Working overtime was a convenient solution to these problems. Keeping his family at arm's length softened the blow.

He drove for miles without passing another car. Las Vegas glowed on the horizon in an otherwise pitch black desert peppered with nuclear test sites. They made Todd feel safe the way a fleet of F-16s made him feel safe. Drones, less so. They were like loose cannons, comparatively. All the surveillance monitors and satellite feeds in the world would never substitute for a man in the cockpit. Drones had sensors on their bellies, not eyes in their heads. They stared without seeing, recording unlimited amounts of unfiltered information, none of which they understood. There was something uncanny about them, something terribly familiar. It was better not to think about how they reminded him of Max. In the interests of verisimilitude, engineers designed robots with human features, to make them more user-friendly. Sometimes it felt like that's all they'd ever accomplish with Max, the behavioral therapy equivalent of simulated emotional engagement. Then he remembered Max as a baby, his free and open expressions of curiosity and joy. Todd had tried to figure out what went wrong a dozen times a day over the past year and half, a total of 6,564 futile attempts. In an effort to avoid his 6,565th failure, he turned on the radio to distract himself.

O'Reilly was bashing the Democrats for waging class warfare against the rich, who were already paying their fair share of taxes. The poor were lazy. Todd finally switched off the radio when a caller from Floy, Utah, stated the obvious. Health care was a privilege, not a right. Universal coverage was unconstitutional. Todd agreed, in principle. But Max's diagnosis had changed everything. Their insurance only covered basic medical expenses, and there was no way they could afford all his requisite therapy on an officer's salary. It was a sad day in hell when family pressures undermined your political convictions. Todd found himself increasingly nostalgic for the good old days in Iraq. His overseas deployments had apparently made him unfit for anything but combat duty. He should have been grateful for the opportunity to serve his country without having to leave his family behind. At least that's what the Pentagon said when they were spinning the drone program, trying to sell it to pilots, to Congress, to anyone who would listen. Todd couldn't help thinking of Max again, spinning like a mad dervish in the living room. All roads led to Max.

Todd parked the car in the driveway to avoid waking him in the morning. The garage door squeaked almost impercep- tibly every time it opened or closed. WD-40 worked tempo- rarily. But it took a can a week to keep the damned thing lubricated. It was hard to justify that kind of expense when they were having such trouble making ends meet. The rest of the family could barely hear the squeak even when they were awake. Max would bolt out of a deep sleep, terrorized by something no one else could hear. It was one of an arsenal of sounds he couldn't tolerate, along with the dishwasher and the ceiling fan in the dining room. He didn't seem to mind every other fan in every other room. But one flick of the dining room switch and he went crazy. It must have had something to do with sound frequencies rather than decibel levels. Loud noises didn't bother him a bit. You could hold a blow dryer right next to his ear and he wouldn't even notice. Rose vacuumed around him when he was fiddling with the rug fringe. But if you turned on the dishwasher, even in the dead of night, watch out. They had been washing dishes by hand going on a year now.

Todd peeked through the garage door window. As usual, Rose's car was parked dangerously close to the bike rack. He had hung a tennis ball from the ceiling to help her negotiate the distance. A lot of good it did. She'd driven a good two feet too far anyway. Not that Rose was solely to blame. Max had probably started screaming his head off the minute the garage door started rolling back. Rose was a tough nut. She took Max's phobias in stride. He could yell all he wanted, but she wasn't about to leave her car in the driveway. Granted she drove a Taurus now instead of the Jaguar. But the former used car saleswoman in her refused to submit even a Ford to the elements day in and day out. Max would have to learn to compromise like everyone else. After all, expanding his comfort zone was an integral part of behavioral therapy. She let him have his way with the dishwasher, but he'd have to learn to live with the garage door.

Usually Rose greeted Todd at the door. But she was nowhere to be seen. He could hear Maureen in her bedroom, as usual, chatting on her cell. Once her homework was finished, she was allowed up to two hours of phone time. She spent the rest of the evening responding to her Facebook friends. There were never enough hours in the day to keep up with them all. She was either incredibly popular or completely incapable of distinguishing between real friends and virtual friends. Todd might have considered limiting her Internet usage if it hadn't seemed hypocritical. After all, he spent way more time than she did chained to a computer screen, trying to distinguish between allies and enemies. At least most of her online contacts were local, kids she actually met face to face on occasion. His were on the opposite side of the planet, and he'd never met a single one of them.

He heard muffled voices coming from Max's room. The door was closed and he figured he would try to sneak down the hall. He very rarely had the opportunity to relax alone in his own home. Watching a game on the tube was a real luxury. Technically, he was supposed to put Max to bed every night. But the process went more smoothly when Rose did the honors. Yet another reason not to rush home from work every night. As he passed by the bedroom door, the word *perfect* assaulted his ears. It was one of a handful of words he couldn't tolerate, along with *scarcity*, *abundance*, and *manifesting*. He should have kept walking anyway to avoid a scene. But he had asked Rose not to use that word. They had a pact. She kept pestering him to quit disciplining Max, so he had a bargaining chip. Todd would stop reprimanding him for doing something wrong as long as Rose stopped pretending he could do no wrong. Come to find out she was cheating behind his back.

Todd was a professional eavesdropper. He listened in on conversations via wiretaps authorized by the CIA. His drone sensors were powerful enough to zero in on men boinking their wives in the privacy of their own homes. He knew full well that he shouldn't spy on his own wife. He wasn't the type to monitor her Internet trail, like so many husbands he knew. He didn't have to. His powers of deduction had been honed by years in the intelligence business. The minute a new word crept into Rose's vocabulary, he was all over it. *Perfect* was the worst offender. Shortly after she discovered the Source online, he accused her of joining a cult. To this day, she still had no idea how he figured it out. He flattened his ear against the door. She had crossed a line, forcing him to follow suit.

"I want you to know how special you are, Max," Rose was saying. "You're Mommy's little prophet. Perfect in every way."

The language of perfection was bad enough, more of the same old crap. But the bit about the prophet was even worse, something Todd had never heard before. Rose must have a new guru. Todd checked the impulse to bust into the room. He needed to assess the threat level, which could only be determined by piecing together a portrait of the New Age clown responsible for brainwashing his wife. Patience was a cardinal virtue in surveillance operations.

"Relax, Max," Rose said. "Everything is as it should be."

Todd appreciated Rose's attempt to relieve Max's chronic anxiety. Judging from the tone of her voice, almost a whisper, he assumed they were spooning in the crescent moon position. Todd had resisted this treatment until Sasha asked him if he'd ever felt out of control of various parts of his body. Of course he had. He was a pilot, a trained parachutist. But no matter how often he jumped, his body was still disoriented by the sensation of free-falling from a plane. Instinctively, he arched his back until the chute opened, restoring his equilibrium. Max did the same thing, turning almost inside out in an effort to stabilize himself.

"He's trying to locate where he is," Sasha had said. "He needs to be squeezed and pressed, preferably in a crescent shape, so he can begin to feel that he is self-contained, a body with a beginning and an end."

Rose, who was not a trained pilot, seemed to understand instinctively. She was a mother. There was something embryonic about the crescent moon position. Sasha encouraged them to talk to Max while they spooned, to introduce language into this physical approximation of what she called an integrated personality. So they crooned in his ear, saying he was safe and everything was going to be all right. But he wasn't a prophet, and everything was far from perfect. Todd couldn't take it anymore. He opened the door as softly as he could, given his outrage. Rose stopped talking the minute he walked in.

"You're a wonder, Rose," Todd said softly. "Nobody can comfort Max the way you can."

Todd felt like a bomb in a nursery. If he blew, Max would too, setting off an explosive chain reaction. Inconceivable amounts of will power enabled him to channel his rage into the dulcet tones of the considerate father of a child with autism.

"But if you keep telling him he's perfect, he'll believe you, Rose. He won't try to get better."

Todd tiptoed his way through the minefield of toys on the floor, none of which Max actually played with. Instead, he arranged them in patterns with militaristic precision. One misstep, one disturbance of his son's rigid sense of order, however slight, and Todd would trip the switch. The whole room would explode.

"When you're finished, we can hash this out. I'll be in the bedroom."

Todd stood over the bed. It was bizarre. Neither his wife nor his son acknowledged his presence in the room. One was definitely playing possum, to protect the tenuous tranquility of the other. Maybe Max was pretending, too, for his own weird reasons. Maybe even the same reason. To protect himself. One could only hope. The alternative was too awful to bear, that there was no self in there to protect. Todd left the room, shutting the door softly behind him.

* * *

At first it feels like her body is swallowing his. He tries to escape but he's surrounded. She rolls him up in a little ball. He likes his shape but not hers. When he stops moving she stops too. That way he can forget she's there and concentrate on being a little ball, his favorite shape.

When he breathes she breathes. He holds his breath and she isn't there. Except when she's talking. She's so far away he can't hear her. He holds his breath and she disappears completely. When she leaves he pretends she was never there. That way he can have the little ball all to himself.

* * *

Rose slammed into the bedroom. It was her turn to be angry. She had always had a short fuse. All the serenity and perfection in the universe couldn't change that. She managed to blow up less frequently than before, now that she was so goddamned grounded. But when she did, the fur flew just like the good old days. When she completely lost touch with reality, Todd purposely tried to get her riled up. There wasn't any other way to cut through the bullshit.

"You could have waited," Rose said. "It's a miracle he didn't wake up."

"Hallelujah," Todd said. He switched off the TV and tossed the remote across the bed. "It's like Lourdes around here. A bloody miracle a minute."

"Let's skip it, Todd," Rose said. She stood at the foot of the bed, glaring at him. "I already know what you're going to say anyway."

"We had a pact."

"Can't we just agree to disagree?"

"Not about this."

"I'm trying to make Max feel good about himself."

"Nobody's perfect, Rose. You're setting the bar way too high."

"I don't want him to think he's sick. He'll just manifest more sickness."

"Here we go again."

"Now what?"

"Blaming the victim. It's cruel, Rose."

"No one's blaming anybody."

"You're blaming Max for manifesting autism. Whatever the fuck manifesting means."

"Nobody said that."

"Logic says it, Rose. There's no getting around it."

She tried to remember how the Source reconciled disease and the law of attraction. There was no doubt it could be done. If Tashi could account for the karmic cause of the Holocaust without blaming its millions of victims, surely she could account for the autism of one little boy. It all seemed crystal clear when Tashi was on the phone with her. The voice itself clarified everything.

"If you weren't so negative all the time, you might understand what I mean."

"That's right, Pollyanna. Blame me just like you blame Max."

"I asked you not to call me that."

"I asked you to quit telling Max he's perfect."

"What's the big deal? Not enough rain on your parade?"

As far as Todd was concerned the argument was over. He had made his point. Further discussion was unnecessary, if not counterproductive. Rose always accused him of not being willing to work things through. She liked to explore issues from every angle, which really meant saying the same thing over and over. The fact was, there were really only two angles. His and hers. Compromise was an action, not a bunch of words spoken in anger. Todd had learned from experience that the best way to resolve a disagreement was to stop disagreeing. He retrieved the remote to signal the end of the conversation. Then he had a better idea. He folded back the covers on her side of the bed.

"What's that supposed to mean?" Rose said.

"Misery loves company."

"What's that got to do with the price of beans?"

"When it rains it pours."

Todd liked to tease Rose about lapsing into clichés when she got upset. Nine times out of ten she took the bait. As Rose herself often said, they couldn't fight their way out of a paper bag. Truth be told, sparring aroused them both. Todd draped the sheet ceremoniously across his thighs. Rose looked at his lap and then looked away.

"You're a real asshole, you know that?"

"Takes one to know one."

"Go to hell."

Her tone of voice was still bitchy as hell. But something in her eyes wavered. Todd took a chance. He lunged across the bed and grabbed her arm. She was already laughing by the time she tumbled into bed next to him. It was the kind of laugh a gangster's moll might let loose, archly acquiescent rather than mirthful.

"At last," Todd said. "A genuine emotion. Now maybe we can really talk."

"You want to talk, do you?" she said.

"It's been awhile since we've had a real heart-to-heart."

He ripped off her pants without bothering with her blouse. Neither of them was proud of the fact that fighting elicited some of their hottest sex. It wasn't even make-up sex. It was part of the fight itself. The nuances of making love went out the window, leaving them both free to do what they damn well pleased. They weren't so much rough as inconsiderate. Todd would be hammering away, getting into a rhythm, and Rose would keep pivoting this way and that, angling for her optimum pace and position without regard for his. It took him twice as long to come and she'd come twice as often. By the time they were both satiated, the fight was usually over.

Todd always fell asleep instantaneously. Even when they didn't have sex, he conked out and didn't budge until the alarm went off. Rose extricated herself from their tangled limbs and watched him sleep, sprawled on his back with both arms flung wide. The expression on his face had convinced her to marry him. For all his tough guy swagger during the day, he looked perfectly peaceful when his eyes closed for the night. No matter what, there would always be this tranquil place in bed next to him. She relied on it more than she liked to admit, especially lately. Something neither of them was willing to acknowledge was getting more and more difficult to ignore. She nestled against him, breathing when he breathed, going through the motions of sleep.

The fact that Todd never suffered from insomnia had served him well over the years, especially in combat mode. He was either callous or remarkably well-adjusted. He never thought he'd confront an emotional adversary he couldn't fend off with sleep. But he had finally met his match. In isolation, he could handle his son's autism and his wife's cosmic consciousness. But the combination of the two, cosmic autism, was enough to unhinge even his heroic equilibrium. He kept breathing deeply, steadily, simulating sleep. One false move and Rose would be at him again, trying to work things through. Even when he was sure she had dozed off, he didn't dare move. He felt trapped, arms flung wide in a pantomime of repose, his blood still boiling with rage. It turned out Rose had been pretending, too.

"Todd, are you awake?"

"Unfortunately."

"Are you still mad at me?"

"Are you still communing with your guru?"

"How about giving me a little credit?"

"For what?"

"Thinking for myself."

"You mean to tell me you came up with that prophet crap all on your own?"

"Fuck you."

"We tried that."

"I guess it didn't work."

*   *   *

Farley's old couple was at it again. The wife came home early from visiting her sister and caught her husband smoking on the porch. His accomplices, mostly traveling salesmen, retreated into their hotel rooms. The couple fought for a while outside, taking turns storming off the porch into the garden. At one point the wife actually grabbed a butternut squash to throw at her husband. She missed and it exploded against a window frame. Pulp and seeds showered the porch. He retaliated with a tomato, a bull's-eye that left a drippy splotch of red on her dress. Judging from the expression on his face, he realized he had gone too far. He ducked into the hotel and they took the fight inside.

Thousands of miles away, Todd's squad was placing bets on who would win the fight. Farley was the only one sitting this one out, in spite of the fact that it was his couple duking it out on his watch. Presumably, it would have taken World War III to blast him out of his vegetative state. Franklin and Kucher backed the husband. They weren't allowed to bet money so they wagered a vacation day. To make it interesting, as they say in Las Vegas. Everyone else except Brown went with the wife. Nine vacation days were on the table when Brown doubled the wager and played a wild card. As far as he was concerned, taking the fight inside could only mean one thing.

"It's going to be a draw, gentlemen," Brown said. "Never underestimate the bedroom factor."

Kucher and Poindexter folded. The others anted up and waited for the hand to play out. The stakes were high. They gambled with the abandon of Diamondback Jack without once looking at Farley's monitor. Everyone's eyes were fixed on their own surveillance sectors. House rules, which were nominally dictated by Major Barron, allowed them to yip yap all they wanted as long as their attention never wavered from their own monitors. Farley's sensor operator, Senior Airman Walker, provided a running commentary on what was happening on the ground, every gesture proffered in anger, every expletive the couple mimed with their mouths. Walker was an ace lip reader. For him, the drama unfolding at the hotel was like a silent movie. For the rest of them, it was like a good old-fashioned radio show. But instead of gathering around a single stereo console they were isolated in cubicles, watching dozens of computer monitors while they listened. Good old-fashioned multitasking.

Franklin was tracking the movements of rogue militia in the foothills of the Hindu Kush, providing intelligence to three companies of marines on the verge of staging an attack. Kucher was hovering over a target in Khost, his finger at the ready to bomb a Taliban stronghold. Brown and Gomez were stuck riding shotgun for troop withdrawals out of Iraq. The official word was that combat operations were nearing completion. Whether the mission was accomplished or not, the end of the protracted occupation was in sight. Classified information sources told another story. A substantial number of Special Forces were arriving to take the place of battalions crossing the border into Kuwait. Though technically serving in an advisory capacity, they were armed to the teeth. Semantics were playing an increasingly important role in the so-called war on terror.

Todd had his game face on. He pretended to be as oblivious as Farley to the squad's incessant patter, the whistles and catcalls and chronically vulgar language they relished with such gusto. They sounded like bleacher creatures rallying the home team. Commanders were required to hover above the fray, gauging what was really going on underneath the devil-may-care veneer, which disguised but never dulled their deadly resolve. Todd knew there was nothing wrong with horsing around per se. It actually served a purpose if it loosened them up. Like ballplayers, they were prone to making mistakes when they were on edge. But the stakes were even higher. With all due respect to the mythic dimensions of the great American pastime, the repercussions of striking out paled in comparison with launching an ill-advised air strike. The boredom factor figured into both scenarios. It was easy to sit back on your heels when pitch after pitch, mile after desert mile, produced nothing but statistics and video feeds. Then suddenly, out of nowhere, a rocket was launched in your direction, a line drive or a Hellfire missile. If banter kept you on your toes, it was an integral part of the war game. Good commanding officers knew this. Most of them, including Todd, had learned it the hard way.

"Where are they now?"

"The bedroom light is on," Walker said.

"Which means jack shit."

"It means they're still going at it."

"Fucking?"

"Fighting. They never fuck with the lights on, remember?"

"You wouldn't either if you were eighty-five, going on a hundred."

Ordinarily, Todd just turned up his headset to drown out all their nonsense. With a flip of a switch he could surf up to sixteen channels, including direct audio contact with Central Intelligence, CIA Crisis Operations Liaison Teams, Joint Special Operations, Task Force 714, and ground troops relying on the aerial support of the drones in his squad. The further up the intelligence ladder, the less interesting the channel. Mind-numbing amounts of information had transformed Central Command into a data processing hub, a high-tech hybrid of man and machine disseminating computer-generated tactical maneuvers in digital code. Increasingly, war was a spectator sport, something that unfolded on screens rather than on battlefields. Whenever possible, Todd tuned into the lowest level in the chain of command, boots on the ground still engaging in actual combat. He liked to listen to the urgency of their voices, the rough, raspy radio connections that faded in and out as terrain, or worse, interrupted reception. He lived vicariously through them, if having one ear tuned to actual combat really constituted living.

For some reason, Farley's old couple also piqued Todd's interest. He had grown very fond of them, which didn't bode well. They might be blown to bits any day now. He kept his cards close to his chest, never letting on that he was joining the peanut gallery. When the squad tuned into Walker's radio show, he tuned in along with them. If he'd been a betting man, he would have thrown in his lot with Brown. Nine times out of ten, the bedroom factor won the day. Perhaps this was why Todd was drawn to the couple. He found himself envying them, a man in his prime coveting the passionate intensity of an elderly husband and his wizened wife. And with this pathetic realization, the whole house of cards came tumbling down.

Todd saw himself as he really was, a man in theory but not in practice, living a life he no longer recognized as his own. He watched himself watching his squad watch events unfolding halfway around the planet, all of which seemed more real than what was happening here and now, either at work or at home. He might have characterized his spectral epiphany as an out-of-body experience, if this notion didn't coincide with Rose's New Age claptrap. He spied a virtual bald spot developing on the crown of his head, a harbinger of things to come. It scared him back into himself.

Todd was surprised he hadn't thought of it before, the kind of simple, elegant solution the military had always offered up to him. He would request redeployment with the next surge in Afghanistan. Problem solved. The better part of him was already there, the part of him that was still vital and intact. Redeployment wasn't so much an escape, like Rose's journey to the Source. It was a way to recover the real Todd Barron.

*   *   *

Rose almost never called Todd at work. For one thing, it took forever to get through security. Checkpoint operators recognized her voice, and caller ID verified she was phoning from Todd's residence. The likelihood that a telephone call could threaten national security seemed remote. But the United States Air Force wasn't about to take chances. Not that terrorists stood much of a chance, given the demographics of the godforsaken stretches of land between Las Vegas and the various national missile ranges dotting the desert. There were more military personnel per capita than anywhere else on the planet, with the notable exception of the Green Zone in Baghdad. Creech was just one of many arrows in Nevada's quiver.

It took Rose almost half an hour to negotiate her way through a series of questions designed to confirm her identity.

Higher security clearance demanded enhanced interrogation techniques. Above all, the process confirmed that military intelligence was alarmingly familiar with the domestic details of her life with Major Barron. Apparently, knowledge of his mother's maiden name wasn't proof enough of Mrs. Todd Barron's marital status. She had to identify what he ate for breakfast, where he stored his toolbox, and whether he wore boxers or briefs. They finally put her call through when she told them that budgetary constraints had forced him to switch from Jockey to Hanes.

Todd was supervising the aerial component of an assassination mission. An unprecedented three of his squad's drones had been ordered to surveil the movements of a senior al Qaeda and Taliban military commander. To the best of their knowledge, he routinely returned home to Bangi Dar for religious festivities. It was Eid al-Fitr, and his compound was filled with friends and family. The CIA was hoping to pull off a raid to avoid excessive civilian casualties. If all went well, Navy SEALs would helicopter in and out, conducting what was officially classified as a targeted assassination. But if Plan A failed, Brown and Poindexter were poised and ready to pull the trigger. Plan B, bombing the entire compound, still qualified as a targeted assassination. Critics of the drone program argued that it was overkill. The commander was a large man, six foot four in stocking feet, but not large enough to warrant a Hellfire missile. Or two. Or three. Collateral damage was a drone's worst enemy, in the media if not in fact. But this particular warlord was too big a fish to avoid frying, one way or the other.

Todd had his hands full and then some, juggling audio information from several command centers, including Joint Special Operations Command, and video feeds on dozens of monitors in his squad. But he never refused to field one of Rose's phone calls. He knew she would only call in an emergency. It was hard to imagine how a domestic emergency, no matter how dire, could compete with the magnitude of taking out an al Qaeda commander. God forbid one of the kids had been maimed or killed. Checkpoint operators tried to assess the threat level, but Rose kept insisting she needed to speak directly with Todd. They had been trained in a full battery of interrogation techniques, highly effective on terrorists, useless on mothers. At length, without managing to determine whether the crisis warranted an orange or red alert, they finally authorized the call.

"I hope I'm not interrupting anything important," Rose said.

"Same old, same old," Todd said. "Are you okay?"

"I can't find Max."

"Did you check the closet?"

"Of course."

"The hamper?"

"I looked everywhere, Todd. He's gone."

The first of two helicopters landed in a driveway between the main compound and a garden shed, effectively blocking access in and out of the compound. It was a tight fit, given the number of cars parked inside the gate. The second chopper hovered over the garden itself, using propeller wind to flatten vegetation before descending. No one, armed or otherwise, was flushed out of the garden. Brown surveilled the rooftops which were, inexplicably, free of snipers. The attack plan ignored the fact that it was Eid al-Fitr. If anything, religious holidays were considered strategic rather than sacred, a kind of camouflage obscuring the clear and present danger of Taliban forces.

A squad of Navy SEALs leapt out of the first helicopter. Under cover of gunners in the second bird, still hovering at a strategic remove from the ground, they rushed the compound. A white flag poked out of a ground-floor window. Brown and Poindexter's sensor operators zoomed in, and the flag came into focus from thirteen angles on thirteen separate monitors in the trailer alone. Elsewhere, in command centers around the world, thousands of white flags waved on thousands of computer screens, generating a flurry of assessment but no change in the actual op plan. More often than not, white flags were decoys in Afghanistan. This one was actually a dish towel tied to a broom stick. Or was it a pillowcase? Whoever was inside the compound was probably on the brink of staging a counterattack.

Todd adjusted his headset. In one ear, JSOC was collating real-time intelligence and monitoring the progress of the offensive. The voice never wavered, even when the second helicopter careened and almost crashed. In the other ear, Rose was in a panic. Todd turned down the volume in his left ear so he could still hear both channels loud and clear.

"Todd, are you there?" Rose asked.

"Roger."

"Who are you talking to?"

"You. I'm right here."

"What should we do?"

"Call the police."

"They won't know where to look."

"Take it easy, Rose. We'll find him."

"We?"

"You. The police."

"They don't know him like you do."

"I can't be fifty places at once, Rose."

"Don't exaggerate."

"I'm not."

"I'm so scared, Todd. What if he's—"

"Don't go there, Rose." He could hear her gasping for air while JSOC confirmed that the second chopper had recovered its equilibrium. She hadn't been this upset since Max attacked the cat they subsequently put up for adoption. Extraordinary times called for extraordinary measures.

"If you imagine the worst, you'll manifest it," Todd said. "Isn't that how it works?"

"You're right, Todd." Rose took a deep breath. "You're always so good in a crisis."

"That's my job."

He couldn't believe he'd sunk so low, using New Age lingo to calm Rose down. Hopefully, she was in shock and wouldn't remember. Otherwise, the power of positive thinking would come back to bite him big time. He'd have no choice but to admit pandering to her. Manifesting, my ass. It was a testament to how worried she was that she didn't call his bluff on the spot.

"Should I call 9-1-1?"

"Call the local precinct. I'll get home as soon as I can."

Todd had been a Boy Scout. He was an air force officer with three tours of active duty under his belt. If he wasn't prepared, nobody was. He had tacked a list of emergency numbers to the inside of a kitchen cupboard. Their pediatrician. The police and fire departments. The Pentagon. The last one was a joke, of course, to keep things light in the face of almost constant red alerts. He didn't want his kids growing up paranoid, like all the weird Westerners who built bomb shelters during the fifties. Like anybody would really want to bomb Idaho, of all places. Or Nevada, which was such a wasteland not even the Mormons wanted it.

Rose was comforted by Todd's lists. She had been completely self-sufficient until they married. Then a whole new personality emerged, one she had no idea lurked within. She loved thinking of Todd as her protector. At first it was more playacting than anything else, yet another way to spice up their sex life. Then they both grew into their roles until they had all but forgotten how self-sufficient she had been. She dialed the second number on the list.

"I need to report a missing child."

"Age?"

"Four. Almost five."

"Height?"

"Never mind his height," Rose said. "He's a little boy. My son. And he's lost."

Rose started crying. She really let loose, instinctively assuming that nothing cut through red tape more expeditiously than tears. The intake officer was unimpressed. He had been trained in a full battery of interrogation techniques, including how to mollify hysterical mothers. By the time they took down all of Max's vital statistics, fifteen precious minutes had been wasted. Rose's tears were no longer primarily theatrical. Completely losing control of her thoughts, she tumbled headlong into negativity. Max could be anywhere. Hiding in a dumpster, seconds away from the crushing maw of a garbage truck. Wandering across the highway, oblivious to traffic. Trapped in autistic silence, unable to call for help.

If you imagine the worst, you'll manifest it.

Rose repeated Todd's admonition, marveling at how crisis can bring couples together. She had visualized Todd's spiritual enlightenment and, lo and behold, the universe had manifested it. The Source certainly worked in mysterious ways. She focused her attention on Max, imagining him walking across the lawn, up the steps, through the front door. She stationed herself at the living room window—his window—and surveyed the yard. She blamed herself for the fact that he wasn't there. Fear was compromising the power of positive thinking.

The precinct had posted an all-points bulletin. Every cop on the beat was on the lookout for Max. Rose grabbed her car keys but stopped short of the garage. She decided to join the search on foot instead, to ferret out the nooks and crannies police might miss from patrol cars. Maureen was on a play date and wouldn't be home until dinner, leaving almost an hour to scour the entire neighborhood, if need be. Something told Rose to leave the front door unlocked in case Max found his way back home on his own. Her higher power was leading the way. She retraced every step she'd ever taken with him, trying to expand the parameters of his comfort zone on walks to the playground, the post office, the grocery store, most of them punctuated by sudden, inexplicable tantrums. Just as suddenly, he recovered his composure as unseen threats subsided. Rose stopped to listen, conjuring up her own spectrum of unseen threats. She vowed never to let Max out of her sight again, not even for the minute it took to transfer clothes from the washer to the dryer. How could a little boy slip out of the house so quickly? He must still be there.

Rose rushed back home. She must have overlooked one of Max's favorite hiding places. In the armoire, maybe. Or the crawl space behind the couch. When she rounded the corner of their street, she saw Max sitting on the front porch with some vaguely familiar man. The man waved as she approached. She couldn't place him until he opened his mouth. His barely perceptible Southern drawl jogged her memory. It was the bakery manager, who was always kind enough to offer Max a free cookie, even when he wasn't on his best behavior. Rose couldn't tell whether the man noticed Max was different from other kids. He teased them all indiscriminately, holding cookies up to his wire-rimmed glasses, one covering each lens, until they laughed or hollered or in some way acknowledged the joke. Then he handed over the cookies. Needless to say, Max never even cracked a smile. But he seemed more attentive than usual. On several occasions, Rose could have sworn he actually focused on the man's face rather than just looking at his round glasses before accepting his round cookie.

"Look what the cat dragged in," the man said.

"Bless you," Rose said. She tried not to cry again for fear of unsettling Max. He hated to be touched so she tried to keep her distance. But she couldn't help herself. He either let her hug him or was too oblivious to even notice. He went limp and stared across the street. When she finished he straightened back up and kept staring at the same thing or at nothing.

"I'm Matt."

"Yes, I know. From the Flour Patch. How did you know where we live?"

"Dumb luck. One of your neighbors dropped by for a baguette and recognized your son. It was almost closing time, so I thought I'd bring him home myself." Matt patted Max on the head as he stepped off the porch. "I should probably warn you. I had to give him quite a few cookies to coax him along. He might get sick on you."

"How can I ever thank you enough."

"For making him sick?"

"For bringing him home."

"All in the line of duty. This isn't the first kid I've found on my doorstep. Cookies make a powerful impression on little boys."

"Just little boys?"

"I've had a girl or two. But mostly boys. Adventurous little tykes."

"There must be something they like about you. Boys in particular."

"Cookies," Matt said. "I'm just the middleman."

Rose's cell rang. First the police and then Todd checked in. Matt slipped away before the squad car pulled up to verify Max's safety and file their report. He had an adversarial relationship with the police, who expected free coffee with their morning pastries.

Rose sat on the porch with Max until Todd finally came home. Todd looked tired and anxious. His initial expression was tentative, as though he were expecting fallout for not leaving work to join the search. Rose had already forgiven him, the minute he mentioned manifesting the power of positive thinking. If only he knew how easy it was to patch up their differences. They were just a happy thought or two away from happiness.

"Thank God he's okay," Todd said.

He leaned over and gave his wife her requisite home-from-work kiss, being careful to steer clear of his son. They were sitting surprisingly close together on the top front step. Todd couldn't really squeeze by them without disturbing Max. He was bone tired and wanted to collapse on a porch chair. His relief at seeing Max home safe and sound was all but eclipsed by exhaustion and annoyance. The fact that he had to remain standing at the base of the stairs was the last straw. He'd been on his feet all day, supervising the aerial arm of the assassination. On a good day, he routinely mustered up the energy to juggle his family and the war on terror. Today was not a good day.

The white flag had, in fact, been a decoy. The raid had degenerated into a fire fight so fierce the SEALs were forced to blast their way into the compound. As a result, documenting the success of the mission was a particularly grisly procedure. Todd had to listen to every graphic detail in one ear while JSOC processed the information in the other. Both voices were unflinchingly professional. Dispassionate. In the background, his own squad was complaining about how they had wasted the day babysitting SEALs. He finally told them to shut up, pretending he couldn't hear his headset over the racket. The truth was, he couldn't handle the discrepancy between what was happening on the ground and in the trailer. He didn't know which was worse, witnessing the carnage of combat zones or being too far removed to give a damn.

Somebody had started a fire on the ground floor of the compound, presumably to destroy evidence. SEALs eventually managed to put it out, but nowhere near in time. Several charred corpses were huddled in corners of what remained of the kitchen. One of them was conspicuously small. The body of the militant commander himself was retrieved from the roof, where he had been picked off by a chopper gunner. Fortunately, he had escaped the inferno, which simplified the process of identification. SEALs zipped him into a body bag and loaded him onto one of the birds, proof positive that the raid had been justified. One less Taliban warlord terrorizing the region into submission.

Mission accomplished. Todd missed the days when the phrase hadn't been so fraught with ambivalence. He didn't question the efficacy of taking out high-value targets. In theory, he didn't even question the means to that end. It was perfectly possible that targeted assassinations actually saved lives in the long run, just as laser-guided missiles did, minimizing the footprint of collateral damage. But the proliferation of information seemed to suggest otherwise. Documenting every limb of every conspicuously small corpse made it increasingly difficult to bask in the glory of a job well-done. Back in the day, the target had been out of sight, out of mind. Even if pilots botched the mission, they could hash it out over dinner in the officers' mess, or at the very least sleep it off in a barracks bunk. Instead, Todd punched the clock and drove home to his wife and kids.

Trying to engage with his family in the wake of torching a family was beyond him. He was sick of blaming himself for shutting down. No amount of training could prepare a man for this level of emotional complexity. He kept trying to muster up the energy to actually feel his feelings, as Rose put it, a valiant effort that usually backfired. Anger surfaced much more readily than anything else. Under normal circumstances, he might have fended it off. If only he could gather Max in his arms, summoning up the spontaneous love buried beneath layer upon layer of protective detachment. But he knew better. The only way to keep the peace was to keep his distance. He resented the fact that Rose didn't come to the rescue. She seemed even less accessible than Max, completely oblivious to his profound need to reconnect. As far as she was concerned, everything was hunky-dory 24/7. She had shut down even more completely than he had.

"That guy from the bakery walked him all the way home," Rose said.

"Which guy?"

"Matt. The one from Alabama."

"Unbelievably nice of him."

"Can you believe Max figured out how to get there? All by himself?"

Todd decided to choose his words carefully. He didn't want to blame Rose for letting Max run off any more than he wanted to be blamed for not joining the search party. They were both doing the best they could. But asking him to marvel at their son's incredible journey was going too far. Max should be spanked, not praised.

"Have you told him it's wrong to wander off alone like that?"

"You can't be serious."

"It's dangerous."

"That's not the point."

"It's precisely the point, Rose. He wanders off and gets rewarded with cookies."

"He's still working on understanding yes and no. Somehow I don't think he's ready for right and wrong."

"What's the difference?"

Rose gave him that look. In the good old days, she would have said something withering, like how for a smart guy he could be pretty stupid sometimes. Now all he got was that goddamned Zen expression of hers. She and Max had practically the same look on their faces, sitting side by side like twin Buddhas. What a family.

"I'm not going to have this discussion right now," Rose said. "With him sitting here."

"Why not? Afraid he might understand and learn something?"

"Can't you see that this is a huge step forward?"

"Several huge steps forward. Across two busy streets."

"You're impossible."

"Me?"

"Max finally shows some initiative. And what do you do? Complain."

"I'm not complaining. I'm concerned."

"Concerned that he's finally reaching out? Making connections with other people?"

"You've got to be kidding."

"Max perks up every time we go to that bakery."

"A bakery is a far cry from connection with another human being."

"He's crazy about Matt."

"He's crazy about cookies."

"Why walk all that way just for a cookie? He could have just raided the cookie jar."

"Maybe you're right." Having made his point, Todd was ready to move on. Their little spat was in danger of escalating into a fight he didn't have the energy to win. "There must be something we're not thinking of. Something about the bakery we don't see."

"Listen to you."

"Now what?"

"I can't tell if you're hell-bent on disagreeing with everything I say. Or just constitutionally incapable of seeing anything in a positive light."

Todd anticipated the trap in the nick of time. If they continued in this vein, Rose would accuse him of being disingenuous on the phone. *If you imagine the worst, you'll manifest it.* A more narcissistic philosophy was inconceivable, as though the universe gave a shit what people thought. Or was it just infantile, a bunch of little girls wishing upon a star? Todd assumed the majority of Source groupies were women, whiling away idle afternoons, if they were lucky. And then there were the unlucky ones, contending with autistic kids and disaffected husbands. Trying to feel less powerless. At least Rose had an excuse. If she wanted to believe Max had negotiated two busy streets and remembered to make three left turns and a right, just to see his buddy Matt, so be it. Let her have her theories if they made her feel better.

"Have it your way, Rose," Todd said. "It's not worth arguing about."

Rose was right about one thing. It had been a prodigious journey, even if Max wasn't a prodigy. For once he had deviated from his rigid routine, initiating what appeared to be a spontaneous act rather than robotically performing the same rituals day in and day out, month after month. Todd had his own theory, which he kept to himself. No doubt Rose wouldn't approve. He suspected that Max's apparent spontaneity masked a deeply embedded fetish, one so powerful Max felt compelled to sacrifice smaller obsessions in service of this larger one. He decided to retrace his steps, to try to discover the source of his fixation. He didn't mean to pathologize his son's motivation. If it was, in fact, Matt the baker, he would owe Rose an apology.

Todd got up earlier than usual the next morning, to give himself time to walk to the bakery before driving to work. He put on his jogging shorts to camouflage his intentions. No need to let Rose in on his little experiment until after the fact. She was still all excited about Max's breakthrough with Matt. As far as she was concerned, it was a turning point. They now had concrete evidence that their son could form meaningful relationships with people rather than just things. She actually called it a friendship. Next thing you knew, Max would be on Facebook.

Todd slipped out the back door and ran down the street a block before slackening his pace. He tried to imagine what Max would see as he walked along. That lady curbing her dog? Probably not. Max had zero interest in pets, let alone their owners. A dog might as well be a chair as far as he was concerned. In this, they were told by his doctors, he was an atypical child with autism. As if there were such a thing as a typical child with autism. Everyone had their theories.

A school bus roared by. Todd was amazed at how fast they drove, with such precious cargo. Their flashing lights and robotic stop signs must have made their drivers feel invincible, like firefighters careening around corners with official impunity. Todd remembered idolizing not so much firemen as fire trucks when he was a boy. The attraction was speed. It had always been all about velocity for him, trucks breaking the speed limit, planes breaking the sound barrier. That little boy had grown up to be a pilot. But Todd had lapsed back into his own mode of perception. Speed meant nothing to Max. He had a fire engine in his truck collection, but its most salient characteristic was its color, not its function. He always placed it fourth in his lineup, presumably to maintain the sequence of red, tan, and brown established by the first three trucks.

Would Max have noticed the school bus? In a manner of speaking. He probably would have seen a streak of yellow, without bothering to identify the object itself, since color was so much more interesting than actual things, let alone people. Of course Rose had figured out a way to see even this in a positive light. If Max's color palette was any indication, he was capable of expanding his comfort zone when he put his mind to it. A year and a half ago, he had had only one favorite color, and a dull one at that. Tan. Now, in addition to a penchant for red and brown, he could also tolerate orange, yellow, and sometimes even blue. Perhaps this little boy would grow up to be a painter. In the spirit of saving their marriage, Todd refrained from pointing out that their son could barely pick up a fork, let alone a paintbrush. Details, details.

It was, in fact, his obsession with details that made Max incapable of seeing things in their entirety. Why see that lawn when you could see the pattern left by the mower? Who cares about cars whizzing by when you can focus on the double yellow line in the middle of the road? It was a wonder Max hadn't been mowed down on his epic little walk. He loved parallel lines almost as much as he loved circles. If you gave him crayons he'd fill sheet after sheet of paper with parallel lines in red, tan, and brown, in that order, sequences of exactly the same number of lines in each color.

Todd tried to concentrate on the yellow lines to the exclusion of everything else. They seemed static. Uninteresting.

Maybe that was the point. They would never move or change in any way. They were completely predictable and they rendered traffic patterns predictable, forming a boundary between cars going one direction or another. But this was probably taking things too far, into the realm of function. They were just lines and they were yellow.

Todd crossed two busy streets and made three left turns and a right. He tried to think of them spatially, ignoring landmarks altogether, as though tracing a pattern on a map. Max loved maps. They reduced the world to a configuration of lines and colors, the very picture of the world he lived in. Todd saw the bakery sign in the distance. It featured a muffin and a cup of coffee, a brown square with a dome and a white semicircle attached to a thin white crescent. The sign itself was hexagonal. It hovered in a sea of blue, which Max may or may not have recognized as sky.

It was still early, too early for the bank across the street or the grocery store on the corner to be open, none of which Max would have noticed. The bakery had been open for business since dawn. Todd could smell it all the way from the parking lot, something Max would have done. Scents meant far more to him than sights and sounds. He often closed his eyes to fend off overstimulation. He plugged his ears, but never his nose. Rose read this as a sign that there was hope for the rest of his senses, that with practice he would learn to cope with a broader range of stimuli. The assumption was that he wanted to learn these things, that somewhere deep down he wanted to be more human, less isolated, best friends with Matt the baker.

Matt was busy behind the counter, setting out freshly baked pastries and muffins for the morning rush. An early bird mother, obviously in a hurry, wanted a loaf of rye bread. Todd let her go first. Then he ordered a bear claw and a cup of coffee. He paid and put the change in a tip jar.

"Thanks," Matt said.

"I should thank you for rescuing my son yesterday," Todd said.

"Max?"

"Max."

"I didn't really rescue him. It's not like he was lost or anything."

"What do you mean?"

"He seemed perfectly happy, sitting out there all by his lonesome. It took a bunch of cookies to finally convince him to move."

"Sitting out where?"

"In the parking lot."

"He never came inside?"

"Nope."

"Where did you find him?"

"Like I told you. In the parking lot."

"Where exactly? Could you show me?"

"Sure."

Matt untied his apron and left it draped over the cash register. Todd left his muffin and coffee on the counter. They walked out the front entrance and past a couple of picnic tables to where the patio gave way to the parking lot.

"Here," Matt said.

"On this little curb?" Todd asked.

"Just past it. Right here." Matt leaned over and pointed at a patch of pavement.

A series of diagonal lines indicated a no-parking zone. Next to them, precisely where Matt was pointing, was an accessible parking space. A blue square surrounded the usual stylized chair with its enormous wheel. Max probably hadn't noticed the chair.

"Was he sitting or standing?"

"Sitting cross-legged. Like I said, it took several cookies just to get him to stand up."

"Was he doing anything?"

"Not really. Just sitting minding his own business. With a big grin on his face."

Todd didn't owe Rose an apology after all. There was no guarantee she would change her mind, even after he told her about the parking lot. But the evidence was conclusive. Max had negotiated two busy streets and made three left turns and a right not to find Matt but to make a pilgrimage to a big white circle in a blue square. The apotheosis of shape, if not color. The blue background shone in the morning sun. The white was blindingly bright, which may have accounted for why Max had chosen that particular afternoon for his visitation. He had apparently been unable to resist its freshly painted splendor.

"I'd better get back inside," Matt said.

"Thanks again."

"All in the line of duty."

Todd watched until Matt disappeared back inside the bakery. He didn't want to be seen staring at the pavement the way his son must have stared at it. When he was sure no one was watching, he sat down. He crossed his legs. The more he looked at the circle surrounding him, the more meaningful it seemed. He resisted the impulse to interpret it symbolically. Max wouldn't have. Abstractions mesmerized him. Numbers. Patterns. Shapes. But they were things in and of themselves. They didn't represent anything. Circles were circles, not symbols of eternity or the cycle of life, much less a sign of disability. A child irresistibly attracted to an accessible parking space may have been rife with interpretive potential for someone like Todd. But to Max, the circle was attractive precisely because it didn't mean anything at all.

Max's circumscribed world seemed nihilistic. Solipsistic. But sometimes, when Todd watched his son blissfully engaged in whatever it was that engaged him, it didn't seem pathological at all. Just different. What was wrong, really, with privileging shapes and patterns over meaning and people? Nothing whatsoever, if circles made you happy. It meant living in complete isolation. But Max actually seemed to prefer it that way. Ultimately, Todd had more of a problem than Max did. It meant a father in search of a son might never find him.

*   *   *

Every Wednesday morning from ten to eleven, Rose had a conference call with various soul mates scattered across the country. She couldn't imagine how she'd survived before discovering the Source. Every major decision she made was thoroughly vetted by her soul mates. No problem was too big or too small. Aging parents. Unruly pets. Getting your needs met. They walked Tracy through what might have been an ugly divorce, were it not for the group. They helped Pam visualize her way out of debt. Rose talked a lot about Max. Nobody ever tried to console her. There was a reason for everything. They all agreed that Max's condition was a remarkable opportunity for growth. It wasn't really even an illness. Pathology was more a mindset than an actual affliction, a manifestation of blocked energy. Opening yourself up to abundance could cure virtually anything.

For the past few weeks, Jody's lumbago had been dominating their conversations. No one minded, of course. Everything was as it should be, even when the rest of the group couldn't get a word in edgewise. They contented themselves with offering advice gleaned from their own experience. Not that anyone else had ever suffered from lumbago. The great thing about New Age cures was that they were, by definition, universal. No matter what ailed you, the Source provided the path back to health and happiness. The first step was to realize that nobody suffered alone. Ultimately, once the journey was well under way, soul searchers realized no one suffered at all.

"It started in my coccyx," Jody said.

"Must be a resentment."

"Why do you say that?"

"Lower back pain is a sure sign of unresolved anger."

"Or a slipped disc."

"Same diff. Resentment wreaks havoc on discs."

"Have you tried acupuncture?" Debbie asked. She was new to the group and had yet to learn that virtually everybody had tried acupuncture for virtually everything. Tracy had even convinced her husband Bob to try acupuncture. The only reason it hadn't saved their marriage was that Bob had an affair with the acupuncturist's nurse practitioner.

"Of course I have. Twice a week for the last six months. I feel like a pincushion."

"Do I detect a hint of sarcasm?" Tracy asked. A kindergarten teacher, she couldn't resist monitoring their conversations. Anything short of *Romper Room* enthusiasm was considered unnecessarily negative. "With an attitude like that, no wonder your back hurts."

"You should try Randy," Jill said.

"Who's Randy?"

"My acupuncturist."

"How much?"

"Two hundred dollars an hour."

"Out of my price range."

"Maybe he offers a sliding scale."

"What's that?" Jill asked. Her husband traveled a lot on business, leaving her free to spend most of her time spa hopping. This particular Wednesday, she had called in from Sonoma. Her wealth might have been an inspiration, living proof of cosmic abundance, if she'd been less oblivious to the exigencies of scarcity.

"Never mind."

"Acupuncture only offers temporary relief anyway," Pam said. "You've got to get to the root of the problem."

Nobody deigned to acknowledge Pam's suggestion. A transplant from New York City, she was the only member of the group still in therapy. Psychoanalysis was anathema to practitioners of the Source, a throwback to the days when the pathology model dominated therapeutic discourse. Jody in particular was sick and tired of Pam's persistent belief that things like chronic pain and emotional distress meant that something was actually wrong with her.

"Have you tried Reiki?" Debbie asked.

"I've tried everything," Jody said. "Chakra meditation. Thai herbal balls. Hot stone massage. TCM."

"What's TCM?"

"Traditional Chinese medicine."

"Does it work for carpal tunnel syndrome?"

"It works for everything."

"Except lumbago," Jody said.

"You've got to be in the proper frame of mind," Tracy said.

"Thanks for sharing."

The line went quiet. Nobody except Tracy ever used this particular twelve-step expression unless they were really pissed off. Needless to say, outright hostility was unthinkable. It caused cancer, for one thing. Spicy language was completely unnecessary anyway, given the eloquence of saccharine sweetness. Thanks for sharing was the New Age equivalent of go fuck yourself. A wolf in sheep's clothing.

"Let's take a minute to meditate on Jody's lumbago," Tracy said.

Even Debbie knew this was Tracy's way of telling Jody to shut up. Dominating session after session with something as minor as back pain was one thing, questioning the efficacy of TCM quite another. Nothing was more revered in Source circles than Chinese medicine. Tashi herself purportedly took chuan xiong for migraines. Out of habit, the group pressed their cell phones closer to their mouths, breathing in unison to focus the force of their meditation. But Jody was the only one who really spent the intervening minute contemplating her lumbago. The others concentrated on teaching her a lesson, with the notable exception of Rose.

Sometimes their conference calls made Rose feel at a disadvantage. Everyone else seemed to have an army of gurus at their disposal. Given the exorbitant cost of Max's therapy, she doubted whether she could afford even the most precipitous sliding scale. Tashi had assured her that all she needed was the Source. But Max seemed to need more. He wasn't progressing as quickly as she had hoped he might. She banished the thought, focusing on the miracle rather than the malady. Even so, she couldn't escape the nagging suspicion that there was so much more she could do for him, if only she had more money. Haunted by the specter of scarcity, Rose meditated on relevant slogans.

Compare and despair.

All paths lead to the Source.

By the time they finished their meditation, it was 10:58. Last call. The end of each session was reserved for burning desires to share whatever was weighing most heavily on their minds. Ostensibly, the entire hour was devoted to this very exercise. But the last few minutes tended to elicit particularly juicy tidbits of information, things no one would ever dream of actually discussing. Dropping a confidential bomb at 10:58 ensured a kind of confessional anonymity. By the time they reconvened the following week, the dust had settled sufficiently to ameliorate the embarrassment of exposure. An unwritten rule guaranteed that these particular confidences were never mentioned again.

Rose never had occasion to unload anything even remotely revealing. If anything, she had a burning desire to express how wonderful she felt, which would have been inappropriate, if not insensitive. After all, Tracy needed to vent about how all the men she dated just wanted to get into her pants, which really only meant she missed her husband. And Pam needed to confess that she had indulged in one last shopping spree before declaring bankruptcy. The guiding principle behind these confessions was a slogan Rose scarcely under-stood. *You're only as sick as your secrets.* She attributed her perennial sense of well-being to the fact that nothing deep and dark troubled the still waters of her serenity. So she took everyone by surprise, including herself, when she spoke up.

"I think my husband is thwarting Max's progress."

It came out of nowhere. No one said a word. It would disappear back into the Ethernet unless Rose chose to bring it up again. Truth be told, she hadn't chosen to bring it up in the first place. She kept talking not so much to get it off her chest as to discover what she meant by this extraordinary confession.

"His negative energy is infectious. Like a virus. The whole family is at risk."

Complaining about Todd's bad attitude was itself a kind of bad attitude, proof positive that what she said was true. She felt guilty, but she couldn't stop herself. Fortunately, eleven o'clock came to the rescue, breaking the vicious cycle of negativity. The familiar voice of an automated operator intervened, informing them that their time was up. She was always happy to inform them that another hour could be charged to their joint account, an offer they had accepted only once, the week Jill's shih tzu died. Otherwise their hour together had always sufficed to transform virtually all of their problems into cosmic insights.

"Talk to you soon."

"Have a good week."

"Take care."

"May the Source be with you."

Everyone signed off with characteristic exuberance, emphatically oblivious to Rose's bombshell. Their offhand manner implied that her secret was safe with them. But it made her feel terribly alone. The minute Rose hung up the phone, she logged onto the Source website to make an appointment with Tashi. The fact that her faith had never faltered before was a testament to the precariousness rather than sureness of her spiritual footing. One little slip, and the yawning abyss threatened to swallow her up.

*   *   *

To the untrained eye, Max's second art therapy session was a fiasco. Sasha drew a family portrait again, one glorified stick figure at a time. The figure representing the little boy was poised, paintbrush in hand, at an easel. The other three, two tall and one almost as small as the boy, focused their attention on his empty canvas. Instead of filling it in with circles, as she had done the first time, she left the canvas blank for a while. Max was completely oblivious one way or the other. He alternated between being agitated and comatose, switching back and forth for no apparent reason. Sasha narrated almost exactly the same script as before, giving voice to the stick figures, all of whom were encouraging Max to paint his own picture. Every time she tried to wrap his limp fingers around the paintbrush, he threw it across the room. The fifth time she picked it up, Sasha implemented Plan B. First she made a show of shaping the bristles, running them through her fingertips until they made a sharp point. Then she dipped his brush into the red pot and started painting shapes on her forearms, circles on one, lines on the other.

"Look, Max. Your paintbrush is drawing circles."

Max started pounding the table with his fists. The paint pots jumped up and down, but nothing spilled. They were childproof, provided the child wasn't prone to violent outbursts. Sasha just kept drawing until she was finished.

"Look, Max. Four lines on one arm. Four circles on the other."

He pounded even harder than before.

"Which do you like better?"

He jumped up and started running around the table. Sasha turned her attention back to the family portrait. She loaded Max's brush again and started painting red circles on the little boy's blank canvas.

"The little boy is drawing shapes," she said. "One two three four circles. In rows that look like lines. See?"

Max collapsed onto the floor and started rocking back and forth, holding his head in his hands.

"Which does he like better? Lines or circles?"

Max kept rocking until Sasha filled the blank canvas with two rows of four circles. When she was finished, she opened her work bag and retrieved the family portrait she had painted last time. They looked exactly the same, lying side by side on the table, except that the first one had three rows of four circles. There was also a crease down the middle where it had been folded to fit into her bag, which she hoped wouldn't skew the results of the experiment. She sat there for almost half an hour, monitoring Max's response. He just kept rocking. She had never waited so long for what appeared to be so little.

Rose stuck her head in the door, wondering if they were ready for their afternoon snack, but Sasha waved her off. When it was time for her to leave for the day, she cleaned her brush but left Max's on the table next to the red paint pot.

"See you tomorrow, Max."

On her way out, Sasha told Rose to leave him alone for as long as possible.

"I'm not sure that's such a good idea," Rose said.

"I'm conducting a little experiment. Trust me."

When Todd got home from work that night, Max's bathwater was the color of Choo Choo Cherry again. Rose was sitting next to the tub, wearing an apron and goggles. Every time she tried to wash off the red stripes painted on his arms, he started screaming bloody murder.

"I give up," she said.

"Want me to try?" Todd asked.

"Be my guest."

Todd knelt down and folded back his sleeves, exposing the tattoos on his forearms. They were souvenirs from his first tour of duty in Iraq, a matching set of Kanji characters meaning *Above and Beyond*. Or so said the artist, some dude from Ramadi, who tattooed his entire squad the day after Ken Matsumoto was shot down. They couldn't even line up his boots at the funeral ceremony. There wasn't anything left of them.

"I'll go make dinner," Rose said.

Left alone, Todd tested the waters. Max let him wash his legs and even his butt, which was usually an epic battle. He all but held his breath and kept his eyes closed the whole time. Todd noticed that Max's paint stripes were less uniform this time, facing this way and that rather than in regimented parallel lines. A couple on each arm overlapped. When he held his own arms next to his son's, he thought he noticed an uncanny resemblance. Then he brushed it off, blaming himself for indulging in the kind of magical thinking Rose swore by. One blind optimist in the family was enough.

Todd gently raised Max's left hand and started to splash water on his arm. The tub erupted into a whirlpool of resistance, knees jabbing and fists flying. Todd retreated, trying not to laugh. If Rose had told him once she'd told him a million times. Don't encourage him. Letting him get his way would presumably elicit more tantrums. But as far as Todd was concerned, they had to pick their battles. This one just wasn't worth it.

"Okay, big guy."

Todd grabbed a towel and wrapped Max up so he could lift him out of the tub without directly touching his skin. He dressed him in a clean set of sweatpants and a tee shirt that looked like all his other tee shirts, a faded brown with a little chest pocket.

"Any luck?" Rose asked when he joined her in the kitchen. He cracked open a beer.

"Clean as a whistle except for that paint on his arms."

Rose looked up from her dicing. Her eyes were tearing up from the onions. "Wasn't that the point?"

"Of what?"

"The bath."

"It's not toxic, is it?"

"Of course not."

"Then it's not hurting anything. It'll wear off."

"Eventually," Rose said. She scooped a knife blade of onions into the frying pan, which was already sizzling with garlic.

"Tell Sasha to use crayons if you don't like it."

"I never said I didn't like it."

"Any idea what she's up to?"

"Check the logbook. It's on my desk."

"You haven't read it yet?"

"I haven't had time. Maureen was in crisis mode."

"Anything serious?"

"Catastrophic. She couldn't find her cell charger."

Todd took his beer and the logbook onto the front porch. His neighbor Fred was edging his lawn for what must have been the fiftieth time that summer. Todd was pretty sure forty-nine times would have sufficed. Imagine having that kind of time on your hands. Fred worked nine-to-five and had two normal kids. The downside was that he was probably obsessive-compulsive. Before Max's diagnosis, Todd wouldn't have had a name for it. He'd learned a lot of medical lingo he wished he didn't know.

Sasha's handwriting always surprised him. The vowels were way too round, and the consonants had way too many curlicues. The logbook entries themselves were short and to the point, a no-nonsense record of what transpired during Max's therapy sessions. But they looked like they'd been written by Hello Kitty. Good thing Sasha had typed her original job application. If she'd written it out longhand, she would have never even landed an interview.

Second Art Therapy Session (9/8/10)

Exercise: *Repeated prompts from session 1 with*
2 variations:
1) delayed completing family portrait
2) painted my arms instead of his

Goals: *1) to inspire Max to complete the second*
portrait himself
(figurative representation)
2) to encourage Max to paint his own arms
(literal representation)

Skills: *1) compare and contrast*
2) copycatting
3) manual dexterity

Results: *1) Inconclusive: Max failed to respond directly*
to the blank canvas
(increased agitation may have been reactive
rather than random, indicating tangential
comprehension and engagement)
2) Pending: left Max alone with his paintbrush
(still unclear whether he understood the
goals of the exercise, i.e. either painting
himself or painting the canvas, depending on
his relative mastery of literal or figurative
representation)

Todd turned the page, expecting to find additional results. The next page was blank. Presumably, Sasha had left without completing the day's log entry. Todd reread the results of the second exercise. *Pending.* Exactly how Max ended up with paint on his arms remained a mystery. Either he had actually responded to the prompt, covering himself with lines. Or Sasha had realized the futility of the exercise and painted them herself, not unlike the first time around. Todd assumed the latter. He was too afraid of being disappointed to get his hopes up too high.

*   *   *

Mommy and Daddy call them Harry and Ralph. They always call everything something. Harry is hairy. So is Ralph. They could have called Ralph Harry.

Harry's tail mesmerizes him. He likes to push it back and forth with his thumb. His thumb and the tail are the same size. His thumb moves and the tail moves. Back and forth over and over rapidly but not rushed.

Ralph has a tail but it's long and skinny. His ears are round. He likes to trace his fingers around one ear and then the other. Round and round over and over. He tries not to touch the inside of the ears. They're old and worn and grey. They used to be pink.

Mommy and Daddy liked Harry and Ralph when their ears were pink. Then Mommy started looking at them funny. Harry and Ralph never noticed. But he notices everything, even when he pretends not to.

Mommy tried to take Harry away from him even before Sasha showed up. She threw Harry in the garbage. He took him out. She put him back in. He took him out and he stayed out. What's left of him, Daddy said. Harry's guts are falling out. Ralph's aren't.

Sasha didn't like Harry either. She didn't know about Ralph. He hid Ralph in his sock drawer where she couldn't find him. Sasha tried to make him pay attention. He concentrated on Harry's tail. She forced him to sit in a chair and he kicked her. He couldn't hit her because he was holding Harry. Sasha is stronger than Mommy. No one is stronger than Daddy. He tried to get up and she held him down.

Good boy Max, Sasha said, good boys sit in chairs. She gave him four M&M's. Three were brown and one was green.

He threw one across the room and ate the other three. She didn't take Harry away then. He ate lunch and took a nap.

When he woke up Harry was gone. Sasha stole him. Like the Grinch. He checked the garbage. The garage. He ran outside to check Sasha's car. The backseat was filled with toys. Some of them still in packages. He hates new toys. They smell funny.

Good thing Sasha didn't know about Ralph. She would have stolen him too. He ran out to her car whenever she drove up. Mommy thought he was happy to see her. He was looking for Harry. Sasha made him match things. Apples with apples. He watched her guide his hand back and forth. She gave him M&M's but all he wanted was Harry.

At night he rescued Ralph from the sock drawer and they hid together. He lined up his trucks outside the bedroom door so no one could sneak in. Daddy found them anyway. How's my old buddy Ralph, Daddy said. Nobody ever asked about Harry.

Once upon a time Mommy changed the sheets. She found Harry nestled in the bottom of the bed. Harry what are you doing hiding in here, she said. Harry wasn't hiding. Ralph was hiding and Harry wasn't stolen anymore. Sasha let him go and Harry found his way home like a pigeon. And they lived happily ever after.

Sasha keeps coming and Harry is still here. Ralph isn't hiding anymore. Sasha makes him sit in a chair and put paint on his arms. It doesn't matter because Harry and Ralph are safe.

~ V ~

Colonel Trumble was in charge of adjudicating redeployment requests. He was an expert on the subject, having requested redeployment every chance he got, even after the dog shit incident. As far as he was concerned, his prosthetic leg was more an asset than a liability. He was more evolved, one step closer to the goal of wedding man and machine in drones and other robotic devices. One day even robots would be obsolete. Soldiers themselves would possess enhanced mechanical capabilities. Colonel Trumble slapped what he called his good leg with his ring finger by way of dramatizing his point. The sound of metal on metal reverberated in his office, making recruits in particular squirm.

"If you're lucky, we'll give you one of these," he always said.

His macabre humor was lost on them. They hadn't learned, yet, that everything except death is hilarious in the military. Failure to appreciate this fact results in post-traumatic stress disorder, whose most serious symptom is the inability to laugh off the horrors of war. Colonel Trumble had noticed a paradoxical trend. Soldiers suffering from PTSD were often inordinately eager to return to combat duty. At least they thought they were eager. Underneath their humorless determination, they were actually out to prove that they were still man enough for the job. Redeployment was an act of desperation. They couldn't readjust to civilian life anyway, which was a sure sign they weren't fit for combat.

Colonel Trumble was extremely good at what he did. He understood that combat was psychologically complicated. And he understood that good soldiers figured out a way to make it simple. Deployment czars like him saved scores of American lives. They were the Occam's Razor of the armed forces, reducing troop morale to the simplest common denominator even before they stepped foot on the battlefield. The more complicated their states of mind, the more likely they'd make a mistake. The marines got one thing right. Best military practice was to act, not think.

The last time they met, Colonel Trumble told Todd that he had forwarded one of his memoranda to the Pentagon, who had seriously considered his recommendation that drone pilots should be rotated in and out of combat duty. Todd was forever writing memoranda, all of which harkened back to less automated, more hands-on tactical operations. One phrase in particular had impressed the Joint Chiefs. *Too often, drone pilots lack the martial ethics that transform killers into warriors.* Regrettably, they had been forced to reject Todd's proposal on the grounds that ethics were just too darned expensive. Congress had to slash military spending somewhere, and ethics were the first to go. The colonel kept a straight face until Todd finally got the joke, and then exploded into his signature hilarity. They laughed it off. But it was a big deal to Todd, one of several reasons he desperately wanted to redeploy, none of which he could safely mention to Colonel Trumble. Questioning the ethics of the drone program was grounds for discharge, not deployment.

Todd scheduled his interview with Colonel Trumble on his day off. He wanted to signal that nothing, not even his desire to redeploy, would ever compromise his commitment to the task at hand. He had spent the entire morning making sure all his ducks were in a row. The crease in his trousers was knife sharp. His boots were buffed and every button and buckle was spit shined in strict accordance with air force regulations. As usual, Colonel Trumble dispensed with formalities, undermining Todd's efforts to put his best foot forward. When Todd marched into his office, the colonel was just finishing lunch. There was a spot of mustard on his left cheek.

"Care for a cookie?"

"No thank you, Sir."

"Watching your waistline?"

Duty compelled Todd to laugh. He appreciated the fact that Colonel Trumble was trying to put him at ease, which made him wonder if he appeared nervous.

"How are things out at the trailer park?"

"Things are hopping."

"Lucky you. The only thing hopping around here is jackrabbits. Know what I mean?"

"Not exactly, Sir."

"Sometimes I envy you, Major. I haven't seen any real action in years. All I do is read reports day in and day out."

"I know how you feel. All I do is write them."

"Is that why you want to redeploy?"

Todd took a second to regroup. Colonel Trumble's jovial mood caught him off guard, and he'd almost been lured into a trap. This was no time to grouse about being stuck in the middle of nowhere, thousands of miles from the nearest combat zone. He needed to present a clear-cut case for redeployment, not because he was disgruntled but because he could best serve his country in Afghanistan. He had rehearsed what to say and what not to say, over and over, and within thirty seconds Colonel Trumble had called his bluff. Now he knew why the colonel was so good at his job.

"Of course not. I want to contribute wherever I can. As much as I can."

"How's your wife?" Colonel Trumble asked abruptly.

Todd almost faltered. The colonel was firing off questions like a drill sergeant, first in one direction, then in another. He'd have to hustle to keep pace without losing balance.

"Great."

"The kids?"

"Great. Thanks for asking."

Todd noticed that Colonel Trumble was studying his face, something he had never done during their previous meetings about recruiting and retaining drone pilots. This meeting was about Todd. He returned the colonel's gaze evenly, hoping to ward off further investigation. He hid behind an opaque expression designed to convey that he had nothing to hide. Colonel Trumble studied his face for a very long time. Too long.

"Didn't I hear something about your son?"

"Sir?"

"Playing dumb won't fly with me, Major Barron. Cut the crap."

"He's autistic. But we've got it under control."

"How does that figure into your request for redeployment?"

"It doesn't, Sir."

"Should it?"

"No, Sir."

"What does your wife think of all this?"

"She's an air force wife. It goes with the territory."

"Answer my question."

"We all have wives and children, Sir. With all due respect, I can't see that it's relevant to the question of deployment."

"It's relevant if it affects your motivation."

Colonel Trumble finally broke eye contact. He leaned back in his chair and seemed to focus his attention on a pair of picture frames on his desk. Todd had never noticed them before. They were angled in such a way that he couldn't see the pictures. It occurred to him that he had no idea whether or not Colonel Trumble had children. Now was definitely not the time to ask.

"Like I said before. It doesn't."

"We're men, not robots, Major Barron."

Todd wanted to say this was precisely why he was petitioning to return to actual combat duty. But once again he refrained from delving into the ethics of drone offensives. He wondered if the irony of Colonel Trumble's line of questioning was yet another trap. Todd was trying to avoid waging war with robots and the colonel was calling him one.

"I've had a year and a half to come to terms with my son's condition, Colonel Trumble. I purposely postponed requesting redeployment until I was sure it was for the right reasons."

"You've really thought this through," Colonel Trumble said. For the first time during the interview, he seemed pleased.

"Yes, Sir."

"I want to redeploy as bad as you do, you know. But they're not keen on taking old geezers like us. Why should I recommend you over some of the younger guys?"

"The same reason we've got four-star generals running the show, not newly minted brigadiers. I'm seasoned. I have more to contribute."

"What if I told you I thought you were contributing more effectively by supervising RPA pilots?"

"I'd tell you that's no longer true. Now that the facility is up and running, my talents are being wasted."

"Is that a fancy way of saying you've paid your dues?"

"I have, but it's more than that. I feel very strongly that RPA commanders need to rotate in and out of active duty. To stay sharp."

"You certainly have your fair share of ideas about how to run things."

"Only when asked, Sir."

"Fair enough. But you're awfully particular about which questions you're willing to answer."

"Sir?"

Colonel Trumble leaned forward. He was watching Todd again.

"What's your son's name?"

"Max."

"What did you mean when you said you've come to terms with his condition?"

"I won't pretend his diagnosis wasn't a shock. But we've set up a comprehensive treatment program. It's part of our lives now. Part of our routine as a family."

"He's coming along?"

"As well as can be expected."

Colonel Trumble let out one of his belly laughs. It sounded ridiculous, even cruel, given the context. Suddenly Todd felt protective of Max, as though his son were the butt of one of the colonel's off-color jokes. He fought to maintain his neutral expression.

"The first time I asked you about your kids, you said they were great."

"I didn't realize at the time that you thought my family might be an issue."

"I can't say your candor recommends you."

Todd felt cornered. If he acknowledged the exigencies of family life, he might jeopardize his chances for redeployment. If he didn't acknowledge them, he would be censured for paying insufficient attention to his son's special needs. Catch-22.

"It's not fair to penalize me just because I have an autistic son."

"It's not about him. It's about you. Guys are always trying to impress me during these little interviews. It's my job to get to the bottom of things. To select men who are fit to serve their country most effectively, both physically and mentally."

"I've proven myself time and again. I'll let my record speak for itself."

"Very well. We'll get back to you by the end of the month."

This time when Todd saluted, Colonel Trumble saluted back. The formality seemed out of place, given what had just transpired. If such a thing as a heart-to-heart was possible in the military, they'd just had one. The entire exercise seemed designed to break down the detachment characteristic of military interactions, with the sole purpose of disqualifying Todd's petition for redeployment. He had been summoned to prove he was fit for active duty and then criticized for exhibiting the emotional resilience necessary to serve—faulted first for being a robot and then for being a man. It was all very confusing, especially when he was expected to fly drones one minute and sit down to dinner with his kids the next, with no buffer except his own heroic feats of compartmentalization. To simplify things, he blamed Colonel Trumble. He wasn't very good at his job after all.

*   *   *

Sasha waited until the paint on Max's forearms wore off before conducting their third art therapy session. Given the results of the previous two, she decided to take a slightly different tack. She learned from her weekly meetings with Rose and Todd that there had been some debate over Max's body paint. Not that they told her outright. Todd made some crack about tattoos, which Rose pretended not to hear. When Sasha asked him what he meant, he rubbed his left forearm and said something vague about Max's resistance to washing off the paint. She wasn't trained as a marriage counselor, but it pretty much came with the territory. She could read between the lines even if they couldn't.

Sasha tried to adjust Max's treatment to address family dynamics. This approach was in keeping with their initial decision to meld ABA and Floortime techniques to combine behavioral and more emotional prompts. She liked to think that Max's interactions were less robotic than those of other children on the spectrum. Her only real evidence was anecdotal, the notes she compared with fellow therapists in professional chat rooms. Nevada was still a kind of autism desert with very few resources available except on the Internet. YouTube videos, which were usually staged to promote one therapeutic model over another, were notoriously unreliable. For the same reason, she took online advice with a grain of salt, even that of gurus like Dr. Stanley Greenspan whose websites were alternately informative and promotional. Like pioneers of old, Sasha had to rely on her wits and the painstaking guidance of trial and error.

The fact that Rose and Todd had argued about Max's body paint was potentially a good sign. Art therapy was providing a common language, one that resonated with parents and children alike. Even Maureen had apparently weighed in on the subject, using it as an excuse to start wearing toenail polish. If Max could apply body paint, why couldn't she? Arguing wasn't exactly an ideal form of communication. But if normalcy was the goal, they were certainly moving in the right direction, one well worth pursuing. Sasha's family portraits were inspiring the Barrons to act more like a family, fights and all.

Too bad they never really argued about what they were arguing about. Their little spats were like proxy wars, one step removed from the real bone of contention. The threat was too terrible to meet head-on. Every time Todd mentioned the possibility of redeployment, Rose pooh-poohed it. Surely even the air force wasn't desperate enough to send an old fart with an autistic kid on yet another tour overseas. She laughed and said she was kidding. In fact, they both laughed in a decidedly humorless way, especially when Sasha was around. They must have thought she was as prone to denial as they were. If Colonel Trumble granted Todd's request for redeployment, all hell would break loose. Even Sasha doubted whether the family would survive the feud. Until then, they pretended that Todd's physical presence precluded his virtual absence. The better part of him was already in Afghanistan.

Sasha didn't want to overdetermine the importance of involving Max's mother and father in his treatment. Plenty of families did just fine with one or the other, either because of divorce or because only one parent was emotionally equipped to endure the therapeutic roller coaster. But Max was equally cathected to both of them. Until recently, they had gone along for the ride in tandem. Just as recently, Max had begun to regress again, hardly a coincidence. At this critical juncture, having a parent missing in action could jeopardize, if not derail, his treatment. Max was like the canary in the coal mine. Far from being apathetic, he seemed to detect emotional disturbances long before anyone else did. Either his senses—including this sixth sense—were hyperaware or Sasha was kidding herself. She decided to conduct an experiment to find out.

Max was sitting at the table, as usual, pretending not to be there. Sasha spread out the family portraits from their first two sessions next to a blank sheet of paper. Then she started painting a picture of the little boy Max at his easel, with his mother standing behind him. A somewhat smaller stick figure, presumably Maureen, mirrored their mother's attentive demeanor. All eyes were on the little boy's blank canvas, with the notable exception of the father figure. There was a glaring hole where Todd usually stood in the family portrait. Max sat uncharacteristically quiet as Sasha painted. His eyes were fixed on some indeterminate point on the wall, but his peripheral vision included the table.

"What are you drawing, Max?" Sasha prompted.

When she wrapped his fingers around his paintbrush, they were limp and unresponsive. But he didn't throw it across the room.

"Let's draw some numbers, Max."

His fists clenched slightly and then relaxed.

"I'll go first."

Sasha loaded her brush with red and painted two rows of four circles on the little boy's blank canvas. Max continued to sit perfectly still. His eyes remained fixed on the wall.

"Now you try it."

They sat there for almost fifteen minutes before Sasha reached over to cup Max's left hand in hers. She managed to guide his brush halfway to the paint pot before he pulled away. He moved his hand as far away as possible but kept holding the brush.

"I'll finish the numbers and you can finish the rest."

Sasha filled in the canvas until there were three rows of four circles, the pattern established in the first art therapy session. She had already added a third row to the second painting, the one she hoped Max might finish on his own. Consistency couldn't be overestimated, especially in the case of children with autism. They needed to feel safe, but not too safe to preclude adaptability. Painting the painting was a kind of play within a play, a way of dramatizing the distinction between literal and figurative representation. Once Max learned the difference between the two, he might move beyond imitation into the more abstract realm of actual expression. Language itself was an abstraction of the highest order.

Sasha toyed with the idea of repeating the body art segment of the exercise. But if she was reading Max's body language correctly, he had already transferred his attention to the portrait itself. Painting his arms again would constitute a regression back to mere mimicry. The possibility that his remarkably docile demeanor might indicate indifference rather than receptivity crossed her mind. She decided to take a chance with the more positive diagnosis of his behavior. They could always backtrack next time if necessary.

"There now," Sasha said, angling the pictures so that they lay side by side in front of him. "This little boy certainly likes to draw numbers. One two three four. I wonder if he likes to draw anything else."

Max failed to respond. Either they had reached a stalemate, or they had reached nothing at all. An untrained observer might have described him as comatose. All of his usual stimming rituals were momentarily suspended. No flapping. No facial tics. He didn't even seem to blink. Sasha had only witnessed this level of inertia once before, the first day they met. She had chattered away for a full two hours, telling him what fun they were going to have together. He had breathed and swallowed and stared at the wall. But there was no comparison, really. This time he was holding a paintbrush. His eyes, which were trained on the same spot on the same wall, weren't glazed over. Another monumental milestone was within reach.

When their time was up, Sasha left the room without repeating her challenge. *I'll finish the numbers and you can finish the rest.* She knew from experience that Max never forgot anything. Weeks might go by, and he'd finally respond to some previous prompt, expressing himself with gestures rather than with words. Sometimes she had to pore over the logbook to figure out what he was responding to. One day, seemingly out of the blue, he started pointing to everything red in the room, something she'd asked him to do two months prior. The act of pointing itself, the first step toward communication, had taken him a very long time to master. Or was he just watching and waiting to see if Sasha was trustworthy? Overall, lag times were getting shorter and shorter. But there were still days at a time when he absolutely refused to respond at all, for no apparent reason.

The next morning when Sasha checked the outcome of her experiment, she found that Max had in fact been more engaged than indifferent. The results exceeded her wildest expectations. The three family portraits were still lined up in exactly the same configuration on the table, yet another testament to Max's spatial meticulousness. The first two, featuring all four family members, remained the same. In the third portrait, a crude circle had been painted in red, filling the blank space where Todd belonged. A row of vertical lines extended across the top of the circle, unmistakable evidence that Max had learned to draw well enough to render his father's crew cut.

*   *   *

Sasha was more upbeat than usual at their weekly meeting. Todd was surprised. If anything, Max was even more zoned out lately, off in his own little world. For some reason, the planet Mars came to mind. The red planet, veiled in mystery. All the hours and days and weeks and months of therapy seemed counterproductive, as though Max were determined to fend off their efforts to reach him by shutting down completely. Todd refrained from conveying his concern to Rose, who was in her own orbit around Mars. On her version of that fair planet, Max was a kind of prodigy, capable of all manner of communication Todd just hadn't learned how to decipher yet, earthling that he was.

"He's had a major breakthrough," Sasha said.

Rose nodded knowingly.

Sasha spread out the three family portraits, labeled Art Therapy #1, #2, and #3, along with the dates of each session. Rose had already read all three log entries recording Sasha's interpretation of the results. As usual, things were nuts at work, and Todd had fallen behind in his reading. Being out of the loop had its advantages. It meant he was less susceptible to the pipe dreams even Sasha sometimes indulged in, if only to bolster her morale in the face of Max's intransigence. Everyone needed a reason to get up in the morning. Redeployment for Todd. Mystic crystal revelations for Rose. Behavioral breakthroughs for Sasha.

Last time they had been over the moon with excitement because Max had managed to smear paint on his forearms. Todd tried not to be dismissive. He even briefly entertained the idea that Max's body paint resembled the tattoos on his own forearms. On further inspection, he had been forced to discount the comparison. Even if the lines constituted some kind of pattern, it was one that he alone understood. They were supposed to be discouraging rather than rewarding regressive behavior. Now even Sasha, who pretended to insist on scientific objectivity, was wildly overestimating the significance of the few random strokes of paint Max had apparently managed to daub onto one of the family portraits.

"Incredible," Rose said.

"Just look at the level of detail," Sasha said. She pointed to a red circle and a series of short vertical lines in the background of the third portrait. The fact that Max had always been enamored of circles and lines did nothing to undermine their amazement.

"Max drew that?" Todd asked.

"He did indeed."

"Anything else?"

"I painted the rest," Sasha said. "I tried to appeal to Max's desire for consistency by drawing the same picture three times, hoping he'd feel compelled to fill in the blank."

"To complete the pattern."

"Right. We started with simple shapes painted on our arms and graduated to these family portraits. Patterns with human content. Max made the leap in only three sessions. I've never seen more remarkable progress in such a short span of time."

"We've discovered Max's native language," Rose said. "It's all there. Latent. Ready to explode into words."

"I'm not prepared to go that far," Sasha said.

Todd resisted the impulse to make a snide comment. At the very least, Sasha was still one orbit short of Mars.

"Why not?" Rose asked.

"He's obviously more visual than verbal. At this point, there's no telling how hardwired this is. He may stay that way."

"But he's come so far already."

"He hasn't come to us so much as we've come to him. We're learning to speak his language."

Todd picked up the third portrait. He tried to suspend his disbelief. He felt disloyal to Max, as though he were doubting his son's capacity to communicate. But he honestly had no idea what Sasha and Rose were talking about. What he saw was a circle and some lines, not unlike Max's round potatoes at dinner and his trains of trucks and cars, snaking their way like minefields through the house. One false move—one disrupted detail in his obsessive-compulsive sequences—and Max would respond with hysteria, not language.

"Why did you decide to leave me out of the third picture?" Todd asked.

"Just a hunch," Sasha said cryptically.

"Based on what?"

Sasha glanced at Rose before turning back to Todd.

"Sometimes I think Max feels a particular affinity with you."

Todd watched Rose's face out of the corner of his eye. He wondered if she had put Sasha up to this, if they were ganging up in an effort to convince him, surreptitiously, to withdraw his request for redeployment.

"He barely notices me," Todd said.

"He noticed you this time."

"Where?"

"Here." Sasha pointed to the circle hovering in the large blank space in the drawing.

"What is it you think you're seeing here that I can't see?"

"You."

"It's a circle," Todd said. "Don't you remember when Max practically got run over, wandering all the way to the bakery to commune with a handicapped parking circle? Back when he was still relatively mobile? Now he's practically comatose."

"He's calmer," Rose said. "Less hyperactive."

"Less distracted," Sasha said. "He's never really been hyperactive."

"He's less distracted, all right," Todd said. "But what if it's because he's less engaged? More distant?"

"Why choose the most negative interpretation, Todd?" Rose asked. "Don't you want Max to get better?"

"What's better about substituting one circle for another? Max didn't plop himself in the middle of that handicapped zone because he was trying to communicate something about being disabled. Surely even you don't believe that, do you, Rose?"

"I think he was communicating spatially. Abstractly."

"Where'd you get that particular interpretation? Online?"

"It's common sense, really," Sasha said. Things were heating up, distracting Todd and Rose from the task at hand. Let them fight on their own time. "Other kids point to things when they want to communicate. Max just uses shapes instead of his finger."

"And you think this circle points to me," Todd said.

"Of course."

"Why not to Maureen?"

They just looked at him, Rose with mounting exasperation, Sasha with studied neutrality.

"Who's to say he wasn't referring back to that damn handicapped parking circle?" Todd persisted.

"Don't be ridiculous, Todd. Talk about making random connections."

"Why is that any more random than your hypothesis?"

"Patterns and verisimilitude," Sasha said.

"Which patterns?"

"The family portraits."

"Which you drew. Not Max."

"I didn't draw these lines." Sasha pointed at the top half of what she took to be Todd's portrait.

"Max lines up his trucks, and you call it pathological, not precocious. Why are these lines any different?"

"Can't you see what they represent?" Rose said.

"No, I can't."

"Hair," Sasha said. "Your crew cut."

"Yeah, right. And that speck right there isn't just random, either," Todd said, pointing to a dried drop of paint. "It's this mole on my left cheek."

"Why are you so resistant?" Rose said for the fifteen millionth time.

"Why are you so gullible?" Todd said. Then he realized the broader implications of his remark, which were not lost on Sasha. He turned to her and they exchanged a long, loaded look.

"I'm sorry, Sasha. I didn't mean to dismiss your efforts."

"I'm Max's therapist," Sasha said. She hesitated before continuing, choosing her words carefully. "And I'm not in the business of family counseling." She looked first at Rose and then at Todd. She was much younger than both of them. She suddenly seemed much older. "But something is going on here, underneath the surface. And it's affecting Max's therapeutic environment. I'm going to leave it at that."

"What are you saying?" Rose insisted.

"We've all got some soul-searching to do. To figure out why we're all responding so differently to the same empirical evidence."

"Provided it's empirical," Todd couldn't help saying.

"One way or the other, interpretation can be autobiographical. This needs to be about Max, not me or you or Rose or the elephant in the room."

Sasha had never reprimanded them before. Rose assumed that Todd was her primary target. She couldn't help feeling that her optimistic approach was being vindicated at last. At the same time, Rose knew she shouldn't be taking sides. They were all in this together. Todd was alternately embarrassed and enraged. He hated airing their marital dirty laundry in front of Sasha. What right had she to psychoanalyze anyone but Max? For that matter, she was a behavioral therapist, not a psychoanalyst. But it didn't take an analyst to notice there was an elephant in the room, if not an entire herd, so big they could no longer navigate around it.

* * *

The obvious explanation was that Afghanistan was the elephant in the room. It kept showing up at their weekly meetings with Sasha. Then they found it in their bedroom, especially when they were making love. As the date of Colonel Trumble's decision approached, it was ubiquitous, the encoded content of every glance, let alone every conversation. Enormous ears and telltale tusks could even be detected between items on grocery lists. By this time next year, Todd might no longer be around to do the shopping. But the obvious explanation obviously only went so far. Otherwise they would have dealt with the possibility of this fourth deployment the way they'd dealt with the other three. Negotiating Max's condition entailed exploring the kind of emotional complexity they'd been content to ignore before the diagnosis. There was no turning back now. Nothing was pure and simple anymore, not even the desire to redeploy, which was perfectly understandable in a military man. Everything had emotional earmarks, bridges to nowhere either of them wanted to go. The Barron household had been invaded by psychoanalysis and its discontents.

Todd was sitting with Max on the porch when it dawned on him that he had conflicting desires. On the one hand, he wanted to redeploy. On the other hand, he wanted to be there for Max. Not that it made much difference. Max was out to lunch, as usual, in one of his euphoric moods. He must have been witnessing something sublime, judging from the expression on his face. Whatever it was, Todd couldn't see it. Max's distraction left him free to study the revised rules of engagement in Afghanistan. They were much more nuanced than tactical directives in Iraq, much more complicated. American forces were no longer authorized to shoot first, ask questions later. Todd wasn't sure how he felt about these changes. He missed the stark clarity of the old rules. Above all, he longed for simplicity, some sort of refuge from too many problems on too many fronts. In war, there was just one combat zone, just you and the enemy.

That's when it hit him. The elephant stampeded the porch. It was Afghanistan, to be sure, but there was an underlying psychological conundrum that made the beast loom even larger. Todd was using Max's condition as an excuse to run away. If he couldn't play catch with his son. If he couldn't teach him to fly fish and rock climb. If they couldn't talk or even sit on the same porch together without feeling more emotionally distant than the remotest mountain outpost on Khojak Pass, why bother hanging around day after unavailing day? He couldn't be a good father anyway. Autism had stacked the deck against him.

He tried to rationalize his way out of what looked suspiciously like cowardice. Faced with fight or flight, he was choosing the latter. But what difference did it make when they had so little contact? Out of desperation, Todd did something he knew full well he shouldn't do. He couldn't help it. Max was sitting there, perfectly content, and he reached out to him. To touch him. Maybe even hold him. Max exploded. One of his fists caught Todd under the chin before he could ward off the blows. Unearthly sounds erupted from his son's pinioned body. Todd had learned to decipher various shades of fear and agony in his cries not for help but to be left alone. But he had never heard Max sound so angry. No contact at all was preferable to the violence of their embrace.

I love you.

Let me go, you're killing me.

I want, more than anything, to be a good father.

Then leave me alone.

Rose dashed onto the porch. She had cookie dough sticking to her fingers, little round treats for Max's snack later that afternoon.

"What are you doing to him?" she shouted.

She rushed forward and gently but firmly pulled Todd off of Max, who remained crouched in his pinioned position. They backed off, giving their son as much room as possible, afraid that he might choke on his convulsive cries. Todd felt guilty enough without the added weight of Rose's vicious protectiveness, like an aroused mother eagle defending her nestling against a marauding father.

"I can't do this anymore," Todd said.

"Nobody's asking you to do anything," Rose said. "Just don't terrorize him."

"You'll be better off without me."

"What are you talking about?"

"You said it yourself. I can't do anything right anymore."

"I didn't mean it that way, Todd."

"Which way did you mean it, Rose? Either I'm useless, or I'm terrorizing him. Take your pick."

"Stop twisting my words around. You're just trying to justify the fact that you're giving up on him."

"He'll be better off without me, too."

When Todd left the porch, Max's screams seemed to subside somewhat. He could hear Rose's soothing voice as he fetched his climbing gear. Everything was packed and ready to go in anticipation of this kind of emergency. He was out the door before Rose had a chance to ask him where he was going. Sometimes Todd wished he were a drinking man. On a scale of one to ten, whiskey was probably a five. Scaling Y2K was a nine with ropes, an eleven without.

* * *

The US Forest Service issued climbing permits for Red Rock Canyon. Too many novices had fallen to their deaths. Rangers actually patrolled the cliffs, which meant Todd had to use ropes most of the time. He couldn't afford a violation this close to the deployment deadline, not even a traffic ticket. He didn't want anything to mess up his eligibility. Colonel Trumble was still separating the men from the boys, comparing test scores and flight logs. Only a handful of lucky pilots would get to redeploy. The rest would have to remain at home with screaming kids and the daily prospect of reporting to work in a trailer full of gum-popping joystick jockeys. A lot more than just winning the war on terror was hanging in the balance.

Todd had only attempted Y2K once before, with Brown. They made it halfway up before night fell and they had to rappel down. It took three hours just to scale the face leading to the chimney. Now that Todd knew the way, he felt confident he could do it in two. He was in one of those moods, not so much invincible as intrepid. The academy had trained its officers to simulate this mood every time they climbed into the cockpit. Fear was a useful emotion in civilian life, helping people steer clear of dangerous situations. In combat, where everything was dangerous, it lost its utility. Rock climbing was somewhere in the middle. Fear was a constant companion, useful insofar as it activated the adrenaline necessary to power through the most challenging pitches. The trick was to physically tap into fear without letting it register psychologically. Above all, climbing was an exercise in compartmentalization.

Even with ropes, soloing was still considered reckless, far more dangerous than climbing with a partner to bail you out. But they couldn't arrest you for it. The forest rangers all knew Todd. They respected his climbing chops. Even more to the point, they deferred to his rank. There was a kind of fraternity among law enforcement officers and military personnel. Firefighters were competitive, always trying to prove they were the toughest breed. But rangers were like cops. They knew where they stood on the continuum of dangerous professions, and they gave credit where it was due. Many of them were veterans, usually marines. The allure of danger had followed them into civilian life, determining their career choices.

Todd dropped his pack at the base of the cliff. Black Widow Chimney was barely visible at the apex of a towering rock face. Pitons left by previous climbers glistened like so many whiskers in the morning sun. Todd chose the most direct, difficult ascent, clipping into the route as seldom as possible to save time. He jammed his way up a tight crack, and then traversed a series of broken ledges to the next pitch. He was too beleaguered to stop and rest. There were too many problems nipping at his heels, propelling him to outpace his demons. Clinging to the cliff's stony face allowed him to let go of the memory of Rose's anguished expression on the porch. Even the sound of Max's wailing, which rose and fell with the wind, grew fainter and fainter. By the time he reached the chimney, his mind was like the blank slabs of sandstone on either side of the fissure. He inserted himself into the rock where the air was still and dank and deathly quiet.

The chimney was just wide enough to accommodate climbers. More sedentary people with love handles couldn't have wedged their way in, let alone propelled themselves up the damned thing. The sides were covered with moss, slimy and super slick when wet. Needless to say, they were usually wet. Even so, Black Widow would have been a piece of cake to climb if there were ledges or other aberrations in the rock. Needless to say, there weren't. The only viable technique was to transform your body into a kind of human cork, conforming to the contours of the column, filling it so completely there was no space left through which to fall. It was more an exercise in mind control than anything else, a test of your capacity to withstand the claustrophobic sensation of being buried alive in a stone coffin suspended far above the unforgiving ground below, where you would end up dead and buried if your nerves failed the test. Todd inched himself up the chimney, flexing and unflexing with painstaking precision, filling the room vacated by one muscle with another, slithering snake-like through gravity itself. The rock dug into his skin. He could feel every grain in the unfeeling sandstone, but the pain didn't register. He was numb to it and to everything else that threatened his concentration, which was ultimately more physical than mental. The site of his being became his body, an inviolable place where anger and guilt and sadness didn't exist.

The chimney was crowned with an impossible overhang. Nobody in their right mind attempted it. Two routes peeled off, one to the right up a diagonal groove, the other to the left over a belly roll. Without hesitation, Todd planted his right foot on the lip of the groove and lunged, arching his back and extending his arms to their utmost reach. He grabbed the overhanging ledge with both hands as his legs swung free. His left hold held. His right slipped and he dangled by one arm, swinging back and forth, back and forth, with nothing above or below to clutch as if his life depended on it, which of course it did. The rope dangled from his waist, more a formality than anything else. He hadn't clipped in since inserting himself into the rock at the base of Black Widow Chimney. His life didn't flash before his eyes. Max's did. A bouncing baby, precocious as you please until his third birthday. The most beautiful boy in the world, blowing out the candles on his cake, squealing with delight one week and with terror the next, a haunted child haunting his father, a specter even more terrifying than the eleven hundred foot vertical drop five fingers away.

Todd's body responded to the threat while his mind looked on, pondering the futility of it all. Instinctively, he gathered up all his remaining strength to save himself, sticking with the gluey tenacity of a spider to the rock. He crunched his stomach to lever his legs forward, rotating his torso just enough to curve his left foot close enough to toe a crack, but not far enough to compromise the angle of his hand hold. His arm ached with the effort to support the tension of so many muscles moving in so many different directions. Four moves later he was standing on top of the overhang, safe but far from sound. The pain in his muscles subsided, leaving room for the full force of his emotional agony. He untied the rope around his waist, the umbilical cord connecting him with his family. It slithered off the rock, plunging into the void before the nearest carabiner arrested its fall. Short of diving headlong off the cliff, Todd could never escape his domestic demons in Nevada. Paradoxically, his deployment to Afghanistan was like a lifeline. Only it and the unmitigated danger of combat stood between him and doing something stupid enough to clear his mind once and for all.

* * *

There's something wrong. No there isn't. Yes there is. No there isn't. His sister wasn't arguing. She was eating. Daddy picked up his plate and threw it against the wall. Is there something wrong now, he said. Mommy didn't pick up her plate. There's something wrong with you, she said. Not him.

His sister got to eat dessert in front of the television. They cleaned up the mess. I'm sorry. I'm sorry too. Maybe you're right. I don't want to be right. I just want everything to be okay.

They kept saying Max Max Max. He wished someone would answer so they would be quiet. He curled up deeper into the place where nothing is ever wrong. No matter what they say.

* * *

Rose's phone conversations with Tashi completely clarified everything every time. But time was a funny thing. Technically, it didn't exist, of course. Quantum physics had confirmed what seers have known from the beginning, which is actually indistinguishable from the end. Time is an illusion, a mere mortal construct. Alpha and Omega and everything in between are part of the eternal Now. Nevertheless, time continued to play tricks on Rose. One minute she had clarity, the next she was plagued by the same questions Todd raised during what he called their scintillating conversations about her guru. Far less negativity was attached to her version of these questions, but they plagued her all the same.

On the phone with Tashi, Rose was able to live in the moment. Answers to eternal questions, which seemed light years away when she was on her own, manifested themselves effortlessly. Tashi refused to take credit for anything. She was just the messenger, a kind of glorified Western Union courier delivering the cosmic equivalent of telegrams. *We must first love ourselves before we can love another* stop *what we see depends on what we look for* stop *we only lose what we cling to.* The truth was always simple, not to say pithy, always capable of being expressed in a single declarative sentence. *Change your thoughts and you change the world. It is better to travel than to arrive.*

Tashi insisted these truths were self-evident. But Rose couldn't muster them up when she needed them most, arguing endlessly with Todd. Even when she did manage to remember a stray truth or two, he shot them down one after another, calling them slogans just to piss her off. He had several pet peeves, but one in particular really whipped him into a frenzy. *Disease is a state of mind.* Todd said it was a cheap shot New Age pseudo-spiritual way of blaming the victim. How could innocent children be held accountable for manifesting disease? Tashi had answered this same fundamental question thousands of time, with reference to world hunger, poverty, and genocide, among other atrocities. She answered it with complete confidence and comprehension. Her voice alone vanquished uncertainty, the voice of cosmic clarity. If only Rose had been allowed to tape their conversations. In the interests of focusing on the Now, the Source prohibited recording devices of any kind. Every session with Tashi embodied living in the moment.

Rose remembered something about technological proliferation and the alarming incidence of autism in the richest, most advanced countries in the world. Something about gifted children channeling sensory overload, harbingers of things to come. Prophets were always misunderstood. But they were wont to retreat into deserts, not into themselves. What good was the gift of prophecy if no one could understand the message? Deep down, Rose had no doubt Max was gifted rather than disabled. But she was having trouble digging down to the source of his genius. She needed another conversation with Tashi.

Rose never bothered telling Todd about her one-on-one sessions with Tashi. He would have found out on his own if he hadn't been so busy at work. Something big was happening over in Pakistan. Judging from his level of preoccupation, Todd and his team were actually making it happen. He wasn't at liberty to talk about it, but Rose could always gauge his stress level by a tiny little muscle spasm in his left cheek. No one else probably even noticed. He was working so many extra hours he didn't have time to pay the bills. A model air force wife, Rose was only too happy to pick up the slack at home, which meant Todd never saw the MasterCard bill with the $75 charge for every private phone call. Plus tax. They were on a tight budget. Too bad the armed services didn't pay overtime.

Rose didn't consider it lying. More like don't ask, don't tell. One of the secrets to the success of their marriage was that they kept secrets when full disclosure would cause more harm than good. The culture of the military bred this kind of secrecy, known professionally as discretion. It was difficult to break the habit, especially when it came in handy. Todd wasn't at liberty to talk about God knows what. In turn, Rose knew better than to talk about God or whatever matrix of forces was responsible for manifesting universal abundance and prosperity. The last time she made the mistake of bringing it up, Todd said he wished the universe would quit manifesting such an abundance of crapola. Enough was enough.

As long as Todd was too preoccupied to tend to their finances, her secret was safe. Still, Rose would have preferred avoiding a paper trail. But the Source wouldn't accept alternate methods of payment, not even certified checks. To schedule an appointment with Tashi, you had to enter a credit card number. Rose logged on to the site, plugging in a password created with a very specific intention: *MAXimumPlenitude*. First she had tried just *plenitude*. It had already been spoken for. She had assumed *MAXimumPlenitude* had too many characters until she learned that, in keeping with the promise of abundance, the Source accommodated passwords of unlimited length. Tashi had thought of everything.

The earliest available appointment was the following Tuesday. Rose couldn't imagine negotiating the weekend without guidance. She tried not to anticipate another scintillating conversation with Todd, which might actually manifest one. Not that he wouldn't pick a fight anyway, just for the hell of it. If it wasn't one thing it was another. When they ran out of things to fight about, they had fights about fighting. They even had an argument about tofu. Whether it really qualified as a source of protein. How much tofu it was humanly possible to eat before losing the will to live. That kind of thing. Rose really needed to recharge her battery before Major Doom and Gloom got home from work. The website seemed to read her mind. She clicked on an icon picturing a flame and the pop-up caption "burning desire." Tashi's voice filled the room.

> *If you have a burning question and need to speak with me now, call 1-877-778-7788.*

The flame subsided, and a placidly flowing river appeared on the screen. The phone number drifted with the current, from right to left, followed by a parenthetical "Standard Rates Apply."

Rose fetched her cell phone and a headset. This time she'd be prepared, both hands free to jot down words of wisdom so she wouldn't forget them the minute she hung up the phone. She dialed the number and started pacing from one end of the study to the other. She was always nervous when she called Tashi. It felt like dialing direct to God himself, the ultimate long distance call. An automated voice answered on the second ring.

Please state your name after the beep.

"Rose Barron."

Her name sounded foreign, somehow, disembodied by the beep. Panpipes started playing over the phone. Rose tried to calm herself, focusing on the pipes' hollow resonance. She remembered Tashi saying something about how we are all empty vessels through which the breath of God flows, speaking universal truth. Then the voice itself emerged from the music.

"Rose," Tashi said. "It's so wonderful to hear from you."

Rose's voice caught in her throat. She had meant to be trusting and receptive, to ask heart-centered questions with her chakras wide open. She started crying instead, almost ashamed that her feelings did not reflect her intention.

"Rose, are you there?" Tashi asked.

"I'm here," Rose sputtered.

"I'm here, too," Tashi said. "Breathe with me."

Usually this did the trick, grounding Rose in the Now. She concentrated on the simultaneity of breath flowing in and out of their bodies, the synchronicity of being. But she felt bereft rather than complete, a hollow, utterly empty vessel. She realized she wanted to be asked what was wrong, knowing full well Tashi would never ask such a question. Nothing could possibly be wrong.

"Feeling better?"

"Yes." To say otherwise would be to attract negative energy. To say that her little boy was suffering would be to invite more suffering into his life. To say that her husband was becoming more distant every day would push him away. The awesome perfection of the universe rendered her speechless.

"Is there something you'd like to meditate on with me?"

"Max."

"How is our little prophet coming along?"

"He's a wonder. That's what I can't work out."

"There's no need to work anything out. Your job is to figure out what you want. Let the universe figure out how to manifest it."

"That's just it. I don't know what I want anymore."

"A very enlightened observation, Rose. It's not easy, really knowing what we want. Let alone wanting what's best for us."

"I thought I wanted Max to be cured. Isn't that why he's in therapy?"

"Therapy is a practice, not a cure."

Rose grabbed a pen and paper. She would have preferred using her laptop, but Tashi might hear the keyboard clicking. The waiver she signed prohibiting recording devices also discouraged note-taking, yet another future-oriented distraction. But what good was the Now if it kept slipping through your fingers? What good was it if your husband asked questions you couldn't remember how to answer? If Max was complete and perfect, why did they need to spend hundreds of dollars a week on therapy? *Therapy is a practice, not a cure.* Rose underlined her transcription in an effort to capture the timbre of Tashi's voice, which made everything sound simultaneously simple and profound, the way panpipes made even unremarkable melodies sound transcendental. She added an exclamation point for good measure.

"People are always searching for cures," Tashi continued. "The search itself generates disease. Focus on health instead. The truth is they're actually one and the same anyway. Everything is one."

"That's why I called," Rose said. "I remembered what you said about truth being a paradox. But I can't remember why. Or what it means."

"All great spiritual truths are paradoxes. The first shall be last and the last shall be first. Surrender is a sign of strength, not weakness. To truly live, we must die, like the phoenix rising from its ashes. Paradox itself is an illusion. Everything is one."

Something clicked. Autism was a spectrum disorder because disease and health were part of the same spiritual continuum. Had Tashi said this, or was Rose starting to tap into the Source herself, as the website promised she would learn to do? The universe seemed to come into alignment, galaxy upon galaxy, innumerable solar systems spinning a design too grand to be flawed. Too big to fail. Viewed through this vast prism, everything made sense. But did this cosmic vision really change anything in the infinitesimal orbit of her own family? Max might be perfectly healthy, but he was still locked in an alternate universe. No matter how abundant, it was isolated. Inaccessible. Her momentary enlightenment gave way to yet another dark night of the soul.

"If autism isn't a disease, what is it?"

"Autism is a sixth sense."

"At the expense of the other five? Max acts deaf half the time. And blind. He looks right through us. Like we're not there."

Rose was progressively distraught. The voice never wavered. It was impervious to anxiety on the other end of the line, no matter how monstrous the cause. Infidelity, disease, and even death were all as one, blessings in disguise. Opportunities for growth.

"He's processing sensory information on a higher plane," Tashi said.

"Then why drag him down?"

"An excellent question, Rose. Try, instead, to ascend to his level."

"How?"

"By speaking his language."

Rose remembered, vaguely, similar advice during one of their previous sessions. This time she wrote it down. *Try to speak his language.*

"I will," Rose said. "I do."

"Being gifted can be lonely. Only you can relieve his isolation."

It made perfect sense at the time. But she couldn't help traveling into the future, imagining what Todd would say. *Autism is a sixth sense.* Rose underlined it twice, as if to ward off his sneering cynicism, which affected her far more than she was willing to admit. His voice vied with Tashi's, engaging in an ongoing heated debate, the real source of her burning desire.

"I realize now why I called," Rose said. "The problem isn't Max."

"Of course not."

"It's my husband."

"Listen to yourself, Rose."

"I'm trying."

"You're inviting problems by trying to solve them."

"I can't help it. Todd gets angry if I don't."

"If you don't what?"

"Acknowledge the problem."

"Live in the solution. Let Todd have his problems, if he's invested in them. Everyone is entitled to their own way. You can choose to live in the solution, no matter what he chooses to do."

"It's like we're living in different worlds."

"You've got to find common ground."

"I have no idea what that might be anymore."

"Little wonder," Tashi said.

It sounded more like criticism than commiseration. The possibility that Tashi might be getting impatient with her was inconceivable. The only plausible explanation was that she was administering some of the tough love reserved for her inner circle, something Rose's soul mates discussed wistfully during conference calls.

"If you have no idea what you want, how can you manifest it?" Tashi said. "You are learning to desire no less than perfect health, happiness, and prosperity. Offer this gift to your husband, who is no less deserving. What does Todd want?"

"He wants us to be like we used to be."

"Translate that into the Now."

"I don't know how."

"What was the happiest moment in your marriage?"

The question caught Rose off guard. It was the first time they had ever broached the subject of the past. In spite of the fact that Tashi knew virtually nothing about their marriage, Rose was convinced that she alone could help them save it.

"Speeding across the desert in our Jaguar."

"Find your way back to that desert, Rose. It's still here. Right here. Right now."

"We had to sell it to pay for Max's therapy."

"Your happiness?"

"The Jaguar."

"One less distraction. The less you desire, the happier you'll be."

Rose could just imagine what Todd would say to that. She doubted whether his conception of happiness would ever coincide with her own, the way it did when they were first married. She knew better than to raise these reservations with Tashi, who would dismiss them as incidental, mere window dressing in the larger scheme of things. Even she had always thought the Jaguar was about desire. All those afternoons and evenings making love. She saw now that it had been about the journey, not the destination, the eternal vanishing point, not the motels dotting the side of the road. *It is better to travel than to arrive.* They were still on that neverending highway, stalled and bickering over who was at fault, now that the proverbial feeling was gone. All that wasted energy, embracing loss instead of each other.

"I'm going to leave you with one last paradox, Rose." As the voice faded out, meditation music began to fade in. "You know you've come a long way when you're back where you started. Full circle."

"Is that why Max loves circles so much?"

"Didn't I tell you he's a prophet?"

*   *   *

The old fart with the autistic kid had apparently made the first cut. Todd and an undisclosed number of other officers were summoned to Glendale, Arizona, for the first of three training exercises. Officially, they were there for routine requalification and medical exams. Even drone pilots had to prove their eyesight was still good enough to read an altimeter or spot an al Qaeda operative with his pants down, as the saying went. But everyone knew it was more like an audition for redeployment. A squadron of lucky contestants would win a trip to Afghanistan.

Todd clocked out at 1900 on the nose on Friday, leaving the trailer park in the capable hands of Captain Frick. A flight out of Creech early Saturday morning would get him to Luke Air Force Base just in time for roll call. He would have gone straight to the base, to catch some shut-eye in the barracks, if he hadn't promised Rose he would put Max to bed. After making auspicious progress with Sasha, Max was apparently shutting down again. He was stimming almost nonstop. He hadn't picked up a paintbrush in weeks. Todd still didn't buy the idea that Max had miraculously rendered a minimalist portrait of his father. But even if the circles and lines he had drawn were just circles and lines, they were better than nothing at all. The most alarming measure of his regression was his refusal to eat anything but round tan foods again. Things were going from bad to worse, back even further than square one.

Rose blamed too many disruptions in their routine. Todd in particular was dropping the ball, working late a lot and skipping bedtime rituals even when he was home. The truth was he had ceased to believe in the efficacy of some of the more far-out aspects of Max's regime. It seemed to him that Rose's New Age mumbo jumbo had seeped into what had originally been a more pragmatic, behavioral approach to his recovery. If Rose believed that ushering in the Age of Aquarius could heal Max, she was on her own. At the same time, Todd was perfectly capable of keeping his skepticism under wraps when it served his purposes. Sometimes it was easier to just go with the flow.

The minute he got home, Todd climbed into bed and held Max in the crescent moon position. If he wanted to get any sleep at all before flying out, he couldn't afford to waste time fighting with his wife. Thankfully, the process took less time than usual. Max only wrestled with him for a few minutes before relaxing into the embryonic shape that allegedly helped his brain to develop more normally. Then he lay very still and they breathed together until it sounded like he was asleep. When Todd extricated himself from the warm bed, Max either didn't wake up or failed to notice altogether, depending on whether the session had achieved the desired outcome or pushed Max further into the nether regions he frequented to escape human contact.

Todd grabbed his duffel bag out of the coat closet and headed back upstairs. Rose was already in bed, her laptop propped on her knees. She had that beatific look on her face, the smirky little all-knowing smile. No doubt she was chatting with her soul mates. Or with her Facebook friends. It was entirely possible that she was multitasking, communing with both groups in adjacent windows. Todd didn't want to know, and she knew better than to tell him. One thing was certain. Way too much visualization was going on.

"How'd it go?" she asked.

"Not too bad."

"He's going to miss you this weekend."

Todd resisted the impulse to question her statement. If she wanted to believe that Max was capable of missing his father, why not allow her that comfort, even if it was an illusion? Sometimes he wished he could believe it, too, instead of clinging so doggedly to so-called objective reality. As though such a thing existed in the world of children with autism, where the subjective reigned supreme.

Todd brushed off the top of his duffel bag. It had been ages since the last time he used it. When he unzipped the top flap, a few grains of sand sprinkled onto the carpet. They were more crystalline than the local desert soil. He took a whiff of the open compartment, to see if any vestiges of Iraq might still be lingering there. But it smelled like the coat closet, stale and musty, without a trace of the high desert wind he missed so much.

He always packed in chronological order, beginning with what he needed first thing in the morning to avoid forgetting anything. He went into the bathroom and started lining up his toiletries. Without thinking he put his shaving cream can on the left and a little bottle of Tylenol all the way to the right so that the line graduated from large to small in an orderly fashion. He ticked off the items on a mental checklist and then put them in the side pocket of his duffel bag.

"I'm going to miss you, too," Rose said.

It sounded like an accusation. Either that or Todd was always on the defensive these days, unable to embrace love because he could no longer negotiate his family's emotional matrix. One way or the other, it had all become too complicated. He longed for the simplicity of living in the combat zone, utterly intent on winning the contest between life and death. With the stakes so high, nothing else mattered. He thought of Max, who shrank from human contact for his own nameless reasons. Sometimes he felt responsible for his son's willed isolation, as though they shared some genetic predisposition to retreat.

"Me too, honey," Todd said, hauling his duffel bag back into the bedroom.

Rose looked up expectantly, her hands still poised over the keyboard. Todd pecked her on the cheek by way of eluding detection. Getting away with going through the motions of marriage used to be impossible in the Barron household. Rose's bullshit radar was capable of registering infinitesimal levels of insincerity. But that was the old Rose. The new Rose was too busy friending people. Or liking their smiley-face postings. Whatever. She abandoned the keyboard long enough to cup his face in her hands. Mission accomplished. They had avoided another emotional booby trap.

Todd rolled up three pairs of boxers and lined them up next to three undershirts and three pairs of regulation socks. They made a little bed on the bottom of his duffel. Then he folded two flight suits flat, one after the other. He laid his service hat on top and zipped up the bag. His backpack was already loaded and ready for action by the front door, next to his boots. His dress uniform, which he intended to wear on the plane, was downstairs in the coat closet. That way he could get ready in the morning without waking Rose. He picked up the duffel and started carrying it downstairs. It was pathetically light, a measure of how lightweight this training exercise was compared to the real deal. With any luck, he'd be toting a fully outfitted duffel on the next flight out.

"I'm going to have to hit the hay soon," Todd said as he left the room.

When he returned, Rose was in the bathroom brushing her teeth. He was surprised to see that her laptop was turned off. When he went to bed early, she usually moved downstairs to continue chatting online until midnight or so, her usual bedtime. The bathroom door popped open. There she stood, stark naked, with a teddy in each hand.

"This one or this one?" she asked, holding out one and then the other.

Todd was torn, not so much between the red one and the purple one but between wanting to make love to his wife and wanting to go right to sleep. Even sex was too complicated these days.

"You choose," he said.

He was too embarrassed to say no. It would have been an admission of something, he didn't quite know what. His failure as a husband, for starters. Or as a man. He felt cornered, caught somewhere in-between, as though these two parts of himself had become mutually exclusive. He resented Rose for making him feel this way, simultaneously alienated and aroused. At war with himself, if not his wife. His fight or flight instincts kicked in again. She seemed to be plotting to trap him, using her body as bait. He wanted more than anything to fly off to Arizona, better yet Afghanistan, with no emotional strings attached to drag him down. But he would have to fight his way out first.

When Rose climbed into bed, he rallied his defenses. It wasn't the first time they had waged the battle of the sexes in the bedroom. The fires of some of their most passionate encounters had been fanned by conflict, even anger. But there was something almost malicious about it this time. Todd dispensed with preliminaries, to get it over with. Rose was ready for him, instantaneously hot and bothered and spoiling for a fight. Her eagerness to engage his hostility was incredibly seductive. He redoubled his efforts to fend her off. To fend off his feelings for her. To finish it off without falling into the trap.

She didn't say a word when they were finished. None of the usual endearments and professions of love. They didn't so much fall asleep as retreat into their respective corners.

He woke up on his own thirty seconds early and shut off the alarm before it sounded. 4:59 A.M. The good old internal clock was still in excellent working order, in spite of the laxities of civilian life. He crept out of bed without waking Rose. Her red teddy reminded him that she was trying to be a good wife. But he no longer knew what that meant any more than he knew how to be a good husband. He was convinced that redeployment was the only thing that could save their marriage.

He padded downstairs and grabbed his dress uniform out of the coat closet. It fit him exactly the way it had fit him ten years ago. There was life in the old man yet. He was dressed and ready to go in seven minutes. There was a mirror on the back of the door, but he didn't need it. Everything was already spit shined and creased to within an inch of its life. He closed the door and checked his watch. If he left now, he could pick up coffee and a roll on the way to the base. His backpack was next to the front door where he'd left it, but his duffel bag was nowhere to be found. If it wasn't one thing it was another in this goddamned house. Some of the rage he'd felt the night before began to resurface. There was nowhere to direct it, no one to blame for the missing bag. All he knew was that it was exactly where it was supposed to be last night, and now it was gone.

He started retracing his steps, which seemed ridiculous. It wasn't like he'd misplaced the bag. He could have sworn he'd left it by the front door last night, next to his pack. When he opened the closet back up, he saw his duffel shoved all the way in the corner where they stashed it between deployments. For the sake of the kids, supposedly. Out of sight out of mind, so they wouldn't have to face the daily reminder that their father might suddenly disappear overseas again. He unzipped the bag to make sure nothing had been tampered with. Everything was in order. He strapped his pack on his back and shouldered the duffel. The heft of it all made him feel strong. When he got back from Arizona, he meant to ask Rose if she had any idea how on earth his bag ended up back in the closet. Good thing he hadn't wasted any time looking for it. His wristwatch ran a minute faster than the clock in his pickup. 5:14. If he drove eight miles over the speed limit, he'd still have time to pick up breakfast.

* * *

Sometimes Sasha tries to stop him. Then she doesn't. He never knows which Sasha will do what. Not being stopped means he can control something. One thing at a time over and over again. Against the wall. On the table over and over and over. There's too many feelings in too many places. Too much of everything nobody can control. Sasha should try to stop everything, not him. Keep everyone in one place. One thing is something and something is better than everything again and again.

~ VI ~

Rose didn't know what it was at first. It had been so long since she'd heard the head-banging, she thought someone must be pounding on the front door. Or hammering away on some nearby construction project. Then she remembered what she had tried so hard to forget, the dull, hollow sound of flesh and bone on impact. Its perfect regularity, like a drum beat, was almost more terrible than the sound itself. That anyone could be so methodically self-destructive seemed impossible. Surely the desire to do violence to oneself was an aberration—a deranged outburst—not something systematic like this.

Rose rushed to the playroom. She rarely interrupted Sasha's sessions with Max. She half expected to find him unattended. Even superwoman Sasha took bathroom breaks now and then. But there she was, sitting not three feet from Max, trying to reason with him.

"Max, stop it. You'll hurt yourself."

Sasha scooted her chair closer to his. He was hovering over his seat, stuck somewhere between sitting and standing, an optimum position to leverage his neck and slam his head down on the table.

"Max, you don't do this anymore. We do other things. Together. Let's build a bridge."

Sasha pushed stacks of Legos toward him. They jumped up and down with each impact. Rose called from the doorway, but Sasha waved her off. Then she rushed into the room and grabbed Max's head. He fought savagely, as though his mother were trying to harm rather than protect him.

"What's going on here?" Rose tried to speak calmly, but the intensity of her struggle with Max made it difficult not to shout. Sasha was obviously upset but too professional to raise her voice.

"He's got to learn to control himself," Sasha said. "We can't monitor his every move. Every hour of every day."

"You used to intervene."

"We've moved on to a new phase of therapy."

"You may have moved on. Max obviously hasn't."

"Two steps forward and one step back."

"You call this progress?"

"You've got to trust the process."

"Nobody believes in Max more than I do, Sasha. But I'm not going to stand by and watch him hurt himself. Just to prove a point."

Max suddenly went limp. He could be playing possum. Or he could have receded so far away, the rest of the day would be wasted. If asked which was worse, being comatose or banging his head, Rose and Sasha would have strenuously disagreed. Mothers were often the least capable of accepting the inevitable pain of the therapeutic process. Especially a mother like Rose, who felt compelled to protect herself, not Max, from feeling the feelings masked by autism. Ultimately, it was a family, not just an individual, disorder.

When Rose caught her breath, she felt chastened. Not so much because she regretted questioning Sasha's methods but because she had belied her own belief in the myth of Max's progress. It was miraculous. He was improving by leaps and bounds. At this rate, he would be off the spectrum in time for second grade.

"I'm not trying to prove a point," Sasha said.

"I know you're not. And I'm not trying to butt in."

"If he does it again, let me try this new approach, okay?"

"Is there a reason?"

"A reason for what?"

"That he has—" Rose stopped herself. The word *regressed* almost slipped out of her mouth. The fact that it was still there, lodged somewhere in the recesses of her mind, meant that she was still haunted by the specter of negativity. "That he's banging his head again."

Sasha seemed to stop herself, too. If she knew the reason, she wasn't saying. The times she exceeded the scope of her role as Max's behavioral therapist yielded mixed results. The fact that autism was a family disorder didn't mean parents were necessarily open to couples therapy. In this case, a single session would have done the trick, if not the mention of a single word. *Redeployment.* Max may not have had language for it, but the concept was enough to catapult him into paroxysms of head-banging. There didn't seem to be any other viable explanation for the fact that his recovery was stalled, at best. But pointing this out to Rose wouldn't make it go away. Neither would all her wishful thinking. Max needed to learn to cope with a full range of emotions, including separation anxiety. The fact that he was responding at all was a sign of emotional development. The next step would be to help him process his feelings more constructively.

"Probably a combination of factors," Sasha finally said. "Not necessarily all bad. Think of it as growing pains. Max's response to the fact that his world is getting bigger every day. More complex."

Now Sasha was speaking a language Rose understood and condoned. Problems were really opportunities, after all. Max had taught her this lesson time and again. If there was a problem at all, it was Rose's failure of interpretation, not Max's head-banging.

"I'll be on the porch if you need anything," Rose said.

It sounded like a veiled threat. As usual, Rose was being passive-aggressive, speaking a language Sasha understood and condemned. If only she would come right out and say what she meant for once. But this wish, which was based on the assumption that Rose still had access to buried feelings, probably gave her too much credit. Sasha liked to imagine conversations reflecting what was really going on beneath the surface. She still believed in reality, something Rose rejected outright, preferring instead to comfort herself with white lies.

Watch your step, Sasha. You may not be able to monitor Max's every move, but I can. All the way from the porch.

I'm doing what's best for him, Rose.

How dare you pretend to know what's best for my son? I'm his mother.

Therein lies the problem.

Sasha's favorite professor at the University of Nevada used to tease her for clinging to the concept of reality, a kind of Platonic objectivity hovering above everyone's emotional experience of a given event. They argued endlessly during office hours, he pontificating from behind his imposing mahogany desk, she perched on the little folding chair reserved for students.

"Feelings are not facts," Sasha would say to him.

"You sound like a twelve-step program," Professor Marcus said. He made every effort not to stroke his beard, which he knew full well was a species of stimming. Often as not, the urge was overpowering.

"I'll take that as a compliment."

"Go right ahead. But it won't get you very far on your final exam."

She wrote what he wanted to hear on the exam and pursued a different approach entirely in her independent research project. The A she earned in the course meant far less to her than the progress she was making with Max. She hadn't delayed getting her PhD just because of him—she needed to save some money—but he figured into her calculations. She tried to resist the impulse to get too person-ally invested. The last thing Max needed was another parent, another emotional entanglement with an adult projecting her expectations onto him rather than letting him find his own way. They all wanted Max to be his best self. But helping him find himself wasn't the same as inventing him. He already existed in there somewhere, hiding from something they would never really understand.

Increasingly, interacting with Rose felt like competition rather than collaboration. They scarcely spoke the same lan-guage anymore. Mindfulness for Sasha meant recognizing conscious and unconscious motivations. The trick was to inte-grate the two. Mindfulness for Rose meant formulating a con-scious intention—a cause—in order to manifest the desired effect. The unconscious was pathologically inflected, a vestige of old, outdated thinking not worthy of the New Age. To the extent that it lingered in the minds of lesser mortals, it was an impediment rather than a source of insight, anathema to the power of positive thinking. Rose pitied Sasha for being mired in negativity, something that still dogged her, too, but for the grace of God. In the face of adversity, it was all too easy to forget that problems were merely an illusion. Fortu-nately, there were numerous reminders online, if only Sasha would avail herself of them. In the wake of their disagree-ments, solace was just a click away.

Rose brought her laptop onto the porch and logged on to the Source using her new password: *YesYesYes*. Tashi encour-aged them to update passwords to reflect their spiritual jour-neys. To date, Rose had chosen *MindOverMatter*, *Perfecti-bility*, *NowOrNever*, *MAXimumPlenitude*, and *YesYesYes*. She couldn't imagine being any more enlightened than saying yes to everything in the universe. Several of her favorite soul mates—Nirvana, Omega, Libra, and Athena—were in the chat room. They were discussing the phenomenal good for-tune of Nirvana's having recently lost her job.

At first I was devastated. My husband was a wreck.

Men always take things so hard, don't they?

Too proud to ask for help.

We thought there was no way we could survive on his salary. Especially since our youngest desperately needed braces. His overbite was getting so bad, kids were starting to tease him at school.

Poor little thing.

Bless his heart.

You'll never guess what happened next.

You got another job offer?

No, silly. I focused on abundance rather than scarcity. Now every time I get a bill in the mail, I just visualize that it's a check. It's like a weight has been lifted.

Ask and you shall receive.

Didn't Jesus say that?

If he did it's because he was a prosperity prophet.

All religions are one.

Tell that to the Muslims.

Omega! Talk about a bad attitude!

Sorry. It's just so frustrating. World peace and prosperity are there for the asking. Will we never learn?

Thousands of people join the Source every year, Omega. It's just a matter of time.

You know what Tashi says. If we build it they will come.

What about your son's overbite?

I keep visualizing him without it. At this rate, he won't need braces after all.

Rose felt better already. The healing power of Nirvana's visualization calmed her fears, which may have manifested Max's head-banging to begin with. The law of attraction worked both ways, as a magnet for good and for ill. In the best of all possible worlds, Max was already cured. There it was again, a trace of negativity. *What we see depends on what we look for.* Better to think that he had never been ill at all. *Change your thoughts and you change the world.*

Then she heard the relentless thumping again, emanating from the playroom. She tried to visualize it as opportunity knocking. When one door closes, another one opens to realms of possibility unimaginable in scope. The important thing was to focus on the open door, not the closed one. But she found that she couldn't control her thoughts. Dr. Dillard said that Max's brain was still developing. His head-banging might cause permanent damage. *Everything you can imagine is real.* How dare she imagine such a thing. It might come true.

Ordinarily the chat room put Rose back on track. Today it wasn't enough. She typed in a request to communicate directly with Tashi, preferably by phone. The fact that it would be their second session that week meant she was vigilant, not desperate, taking full advantage of her spiritual program. A pop-up window appeared on the horizon of a glorious seascape, requesting Rose's credit card information.

#5732 4021 6066 7414   Expiration 11/12   Security 762

Orchestral music swelled as the website processed Rose's payment, almost drowning out the drumming of Max's head.

Transaction Denied: Insufficient Funds

There must have been some mistake, probably a transposed number or two. The last time Rose checked, their MasterCard had $250 left, enough for several sessions with Tashi. She retyped her information.

#5732 4021 6066 7414   Expiration 11/12   Security 762

Rose clicked on the volume icon while she waited for verification. It was already turned all the way up, and she could still hear Max. She couldn't imagine how Sasha withstood days like this. Her therapeutic distance seemed callous, if not sadistic.

Transaction Denied: Insufficient Funds

Rose panicked. She returned to the request menu and clicked on the Urgent option, something she had only done once before when Todd first announced his intention to request redeployment. Another credit card prompt appeared. At the bottom, in fine print, a telephone number promised to address technical difficulties. Her laptop almost fell to the floor as she grabbed her cell phone. An actual person answered immediately. It took a real, as opposed to automated, operator to field questions about money.

"I'm trying to reach Tashi," Rose said.

"Have you filled out a request?"

"My credit card won't go through."

"What seems to be the problem?"

"It says I've reached my limit."

"I'm afraid you'll have to call your bank."

"Please help me. I'm desperate."

The voice, which had been relatively businesslike, assumed a more helpful tone.

"Do you have another card?"

"Will you take a check?"

"Only credit or debit."

"But Tashi knows me."

"Of course she does. Try another card."

"Please. Just tell her it's me. Rose Barron. I'm sure she'll make an exception."

The tone of voice shifted yet again, this time taking on a mellifluous cadence as though channeling Tashi herself.

"Making an exception would just enable you."

"I don't understand."

"Negative thoughts are blocking the flow of money into your life."

"I'm sure it's just a computer glitch."

"Manifesting money is the first step to manifesting everything else. Call back when you're ready to take the first step."

The line clicked and celestial Muzak started playing over the phone. The universe had put Rose on hold. She felt like Dorothy repulsed by the Great Oz, a pitiful supplicant pounding on the palace door, echoing the futility of the banging banging banging of Max's head in the next room. No one was answering. She was dangerously close to suffering the same terrible epiphany that robbed the Emerald City of its luster. In the absence of Tashi's soothing voice, she could hear Todd's scathing skepticism. Or was it candor? The yellow brick road was paved with gold, which should have been a dead giveaway. The Source was a business, a source of profit, and Tashi was yet another sham wizard wheeling and dealing behind a makeshift curtain. The great debate between her husband and her guru had finally concluded, yielding a surprising outcome. The year of magical thinking was over.

That such a flimsy house of cards had stood for so long seemed no less incredible than the fact that it collapsed so quickly. Utterly bereft, Rose had no idea what to do next. She stared at the cell phone in her hand and the computer on her lap. For the better part of a year, they had connected her to a virtual utopia. Her lifelines had been cut by something as trivial as a transaction denied. What if her call had gone through? She would have clung to Tashi's every word for another hour. The sound of the wizard's voice would have drowned out her son's voiceless anguish for another afternoon. Now there was nothing to listen to but Max.

*　*　*

Todd felt confident that he had performed well at his first redeployment audition in Arizona, and he was all jazzed up for the second. He did have one regret, though, which he hoped to rectify this time around. There was no excuse for the way he'd treated Rose the night before he flew out last time. Taking leave of your wife was a time-honored military ritual, an attribute of conduct becoming an air force officer. Everything was ready for takeoff again. His duffel bag, backpack, and boots were lined up next to the front door. All that remained was the fond farewell.

Not that Rose had said anything. Everything was perfectly normal when he returned home, still flying high from the adrenaline rush of executing actual combat maneuvers in actual F-16 Fighting Falcons. Being back in the cockpit was like breathing fresh air after months imprisoned in a cave. He hesitated to talk about it with Rose. She used to love hearing him talk about flying. A sports car aficionado, she understood the allure of speed. But now the subject was fraught with abandonment issues. These were her words, not his, which she pretended pertained exclusively to the kids. The fact that she couldn't share the excitement of his weekend drove another wedge between them, which was also perfectly normal at this point. Normal was flying robots all day and coming home to an autistic son and an estranged New Age wife. And she wondered why he wanted to redeploy.

Rose was already upstairs, just sitting in bed. Something seemed strange. Out of place. An uncanny silence filled the room. He looked around, trying to locate the source, as though silence emanated from the presence rather than the absence of something. Then it dawned on him. Todd couldn't remember the last time he'd seen Rose idle this way, her hands at rest rather than typing maniacally on her laptop. He was embarrassed to admit that he was jealous of her love affair with prosperity and abundance, the virtual life she seemed to prefer to his actual company. Serendipity. He was contrite and she wasn't preoccupied, for once. It would do them both good to have an amorous leave-taking.

He crawled into bed and opened his arms. They lay there, nestled against one another, breathing in the silence. Todd started playing with her hair, which either he or she loved more than almost anything in the world. They had been married so long they couldn't remember who enjoyed it more. Rose seemed to melt into him. But when he tried to kiss her, she turned away.

"I can't bear it anymore, Todd."

"Bear what?"

"Anything. Everything. Certainly not this."

He assumed she was referring to his deployment. He had expected as much, the bereft wife lamenting her husband's departure. It was part of the ritual, the prelude to a soldier's passionate promise to return home safely.

"We don't even know if I'm going yet," he said.

"You'll go. You always do."

"I'll be back, baby," he said.

"I can't cope. It's too much."

Todd listened in disbelief. There was a sadness in her voice, a depth of feeling that revived an ancient memory of his wife before she had been abducted by her slaphappy soul sisters. A prehistoric time when she could still feel pain and disappointment. He should have been relieved by the promise of the return of the woman he had married. But she sounded so defeated.

"What's going on, Rose?"

"Atlas shrugged."

She hadn't used this expression since her mother died, and the weight of the world threatened to crush her.

"Did something happen?"

"Nothing new. I guess it all just caught up with me."

She tried to think of a way to explain without making a mockery of herself. For months on end, she had spent every waking minute clinging to the belief that the power of positive thinking could heal everything—her son's illness, her failing marriage, the overwhelming guilt she felt as a wife and mother. Never, not for a single minute, had Todd entertained the possibility that what she believed in might be true. How could she express her devastation without proving him right? He wouldn't have gloated or anything petty like that. But his way of seeing the world was unbearable. Seeing autism for what it was, a debilitating disease. Watching it infect their love.

"I don't know how you live this way," she said finally.

"What way?"

"Without illusions. I can't do it."

It turned out she was more of an escapist than he was, utterly incapable of accepting the facts on the ground, as he would put it. Utterly devastated by them. She understood completely why he wanted to redeploy.

He felt an overwhelming desire to comfort her. She had finally shed the armor of euphoric insensitivity she had donned to protect herself. She seemed human again. Accessible. He gathered her in his arms, eager to be the husband he had failed to be these many months.

"Just hold me, Todd."

There was a place for this, too, in the ritual of leave-taking. The bereft wife in need of comfort. Channeling the magnitude of his feeling into a gentle embrace did nothing to diminish its force. When he was sure she was asleep, he extricated his limbs from hers, lingering on every point of contact. The soft contours of her body left a hard imprint on his. He stood above her, gripping himself in both hands, watching the rise and fall of her breasts as she breathed. He was far too aroused to sleep without letting desire have its way with him. To avoid waking Rose, he carried himself downstairs to the couch, imagining that she was waiting for him there. She would have pushed him back on the cushions. She would have straddled him and made him work for it.

Todd heard someone on the stairs. He eased up a little, hoping that his fantasies had conjured Rose in the flesh. It wouldn't have been the first time. They used to be telepathic, thinking of each other the same way the same hours of the day, even oceans away. The tread was light. The third stair creaked, as usual, but not as loud as it would have if an adult were descending. Todd tried to find something to cover himself, but it was too late. A tousle-haired child shuffled into the living room. The little tan dinosaur on his pajamas was barely visible in the dim light. At least it was Max rather than Maureen. Todd pulled his tee shirt down as far as possible. Talk about coitus interruptus. He breathed deeply, as quietly as possible, trying to avoid detection and calm himself down.

Fortunately, Max was focused on something else. No one could concentrate more intently on one thing to the exclusion of all others than good old Max. A bomb could explode without distracting him. With the air of a man with a mission, he made a beeline for the front door. Max's back was to him, so Todd couldn't figure out what he was doing at first. He bent over, braced himself, and pulled with all his might. Suddenly his grip slipped, and he fell flat on his ass. He picked himself up and tried another angle. This time Todd could see him grab a handle on the duffel bag, the one at the far end, which apparently provided better leverage than the middle one. The bag budged an inch or two. Max braced himself and pulled again, gaining almost a foot this time. He was getting the hang of it. Time after time he pitted the heft of his body against the weight of the bag until he had pulled it halfway across the room. Then he seemed to abandon it, walking back in the direction of the staircase. Todd assumed he had run out of steam.

Max headed left instead of right, opening the door of the coat closet rather than retreating back upstairs. Todd had underestimated the unwavering intensity of his resolve, one of the best and worst attributes of his autism. Max pulled up his pajama bottoms, which had slipped halfway off his little butt. Then he resumed his epic struggle with the duffel bag. He was panting by now. He started losing his grip more often, tipping over backward time and time again. Todd felt sorry for him and wanted to help. But this was Max's feat of strength, not his.

For months on end, Todd had been arguing with Rose and Sasha, insisting that they were reading into Max's actions. The parking circle incident. The family portraits. His son's motives seemed too inscrutable to bear the interpretive weight of their fairy tale scenarios. By the time Max had successfully stowed the duffel bag back in the closet, Todd had ruled out the possibility that this was just another random act. A narrative began to emerge, a series of meaningful gestures that transformed make-believe into reality. When he finally realized what his son was trying to accomplish, Todd was overwhelmed with conflicting emotions. Disbelief. Pride. Guilt. A father's desire to honor his son's quest.

*   *   *

Once a week, Sasha hauled out painting supplies hoping to entice Max back into art therapy. She tried everything, retracing the process that had yielded such promising results before. Tattooing his arms with lines produced no reaction whatsoever. Family portraits with or without Todd were met with blank stares, at best. Usually he didn't even deign to look at them. She even drew a picture of Ralph and Harry, just to see if she could get a rise out of him. If Sasha said so herself, the likenesses were remarkable, Harry all scruffy and Ralph with that long skinny tail of his. They might as well have been Tom, Dick, and Harry for all Max cared. Looking out the window was apparently much more interesting.

Then wham. One day he picked up his brush again. That's the way it was with Max. He progressed in leaps and bounds or not at all, with nothing in between. He seemed to store things up, stockpiling them until he was good and ready to respond. The challenge was figuring out the catalyst, if there was one. Sometimes Sasha thought it just took time for him to filter out things nobody else even noticed, in which case the lag time reflected heightened rather than impaired faculties. His powers of perception were so acute, he catalogued a hundred precise details for every one or two random features observed by so-called normal people. Odors, sounds, and textures. Patterns within patterns. He wasn't simple or slow. If anything, he was too observant to function at the same speed as everyone else.

What was true of his perceptive faculties was even more true of his emotions. He felt too much rather than too little. Some of his most apparently regressive behaviors were actually strategies designed to help process overwhelming fears of being annihilated by the force of his feelings. He was like a hibernating animal protecting himself from perceived tempests raging beyond the confines of his den, a mental space small and spare enough to feel safe. Any step outside of this autistic haven was a step in the right direction. Sasha was learning to measure his progress in a less linear fashion. Even his recent bout of head-banging suggested he was experiencing more complex emotions, which he had not yet learned to express. Two steps forward and one step back. It was no accident that the banging stopped when he picked up his paintbrush.

Sasha prided herself on devising innovative exercises. But there was no way of knowing whether her strategies actually contributed to Max's decision to start painting again. It was equally possible he simply had something important to say that day, quite apart from her repeated attempts to find a common language. For two weeks running, Sasha drew a series of three portraits, each with three family members. Someone was conspicuously absent in each painting, first Maureen and then Rose and then Todd. She drew them in the same order each week, trying to appeal to Max's predilection for patterns. When she finished, she lined them all up in front of him, six paintings that might have been called her missing persons series. Setting up the exercise took longer than expected, but they still had almost an hour before lunch. She sat back in her chair, prepared to wait until their session was over for him to respond.

Max was staring out the window, as usual, but his eyes weren't glazed over. Suddenly, he grabbed his brush and dipped it in red paint. Without seeming to look at any of the other portraits, he focused his attention on one of the two paintings with big blank spaces reserved for Todd. For some reason, he chose the one farther away from where he was sitting, even though he had to stand up to reach it. He drew a circle first, slowly and carefully, and then a series of short vertical lines around the top perimeter. When he finished he stared out the window again, still gripping his brush.

Sasha waited a good ten minutes before making her next move. She needed to use a soft touch. Max hated to be pushed. She stacked up the other four portraits, the ones missing Maureen and Rose, and stashed them in a corner of the room, as if to agree they were of no interest whatsoever. Then she sat back down and pondered the remaining pair. She intended to stay there all afternoon, if necessary, using the focus of her attention as a visual prompt. Lunch be damned. She was banking on the assumption that Max wouldn't be able to tolerate the discrepancy between the two—one already finished, with his father's crew cut filling the void, and the other still blank where it mattered most. Max ultimately proved her both right and wrong.

After only fifteen minutes, Max dipped his brush again, this time in brown. He stooped over the second portrait and painted two long lines and two short ones, what turned out to be a rectangle standing on end in the place where his father belonged. Then he drew two semicircles, one in the middle of the rectangle and one on the far end, what might have been a nose and a foot if the rectangle had been a person. When he finished he resumed staring out the window as though nothing had happened.

Sasha couldn't believe it. Max had never drawn a rectangle. More to the point, he had never deviated from a pattern. The majority of the energy he expended, both mentally and physically, was focused on maintaining consistency and order. Wearing the same tan clothes, eating the same round foods, lining up trucks or Legos or whatever else needed to be lined up, counting everything every step of the way to make sure nothing eluded his control. Sasha had no idea what the rectangle represented, if anything, but it wasn't a circle or a line. Whether it was representational or purely abstract, the rectangle constituted a major step away from uniformity, toward something more recognizably human on the spectrum. If Max could embrace variation, there was a chance he could ultimately learn to tolerate unpredictability, the final frontier separating children with autism from living normal, chaotic lives.

* * *

Rose seemed uncharacteristically flat at their weekly meeting. Sasha had never seen her this way, bordering on depressed, if such a mood existed on her emotional palette. Rose was always so upbeat, all the more so when Todd was particularly bummed out. They were either a wonderful couple, balancing each other productively, or they were engaged in a destructive tug-of-war, in which case Max was the rope. Neither one of them would prevail. The fact that their son's relative progress or regression had become the focal point of their marriage meant that autism had the upper hand. It was tearing the family apart.

Sasha wondered what Todd thought he could gain by being so pessimistic about Max's recovery. She knew he was unconsciously compensating for Rose's blind optimism. This was common practice, a way for parents to protect themselves from disappointment. His impending redeployment put another spin on what was becoming an increasingly complex emotional matrix. It begged a chicken and egg question as to whether he wanted to redeploy to escape Max's halting recovery or whether the halting recovery provided the excuse he needed to justify redeployment. If there was one thing her MA in psychology had taught Sasha, beyond the fact that the profession as a whole was alarmingly misguided, it was that emotional conflicts were always ambivalent, with chickens and eggs enough to fill an entire hen coop. Negotiating weekly meetings with Rose and Todd was like walking on eggshells.

"Good news," Sasha said.

"I could use some," Rose said.

Todd just sat there. Rose had stolen his curmudgeonly line, and there was nothing left to say.

Sasha shuffled through Max's art therapy portfolio. She pulled out the two most recent family portraits and placed them side by side on the table. Rose stared blankly at the one with the circle and lines occupying the father's position. She wasn't entirely sure she still had the energy to believe the little vertical strokes of paint really represented Todd's crew cut. They seemed more random than before, more like the lines Max had painted on his arms, which testified to improvements in manual dexterity but very little else. Meaning was in the eyes of the beholder. Sometimes a cigar was just a cigar.

Todd focused his attention on the shape Max had drawn in the second portrait. It took him a minute to realize it wasn't just a rectangle. The little semicircles in the middle and on the upper end spoke volumes, utilitarian flourishes that translated form into function. At first he thought Sasha was trying to trick them. But that was impossible. She couldn't possibly understand the significance of these particular shapes. Todd alone was privy to their meaning, which was both literal and figurative.

"Max drew this?" Todd asked.

"Both of them," Sasha said. "He's painting again."

"He's never drawn a rectangle before."

Rose perked up slightly. "Could this mean something?"

"I'm not sure," Sasha said. "But he's expanding his vocabulary, even if they're just shapes."

"Has he painted arcs before?" Todd pointed at the semicircles.

"Never. Just circles and lines."

"Which one did he draw first? The circle or the rectangle?"

"The circle."

"What difference does it make?" Rose said.

Todd picked up the first portrait. Half a dozen art therapy sessions had yielded the same circle with vertical lines sprouting out of the top. It was either evidence of yet another obsessive-compulsive pattern, an autistic barrier erected to prevent communication with his family. Or it was Max's way of acknowledging that he was actually part of the family, something that Todd himself found increasingly difficult to feel, let alone express. The rectangle cracked the code, confirming the latter interpretation. It was no longer possible to see the circles and lines as anything but a father figure.

"You've been right all along," Todd said.

"What do you mean?"

"They're not just shapes." Todd traced the image in the second portrait with his index finger. He tried to feel what Max must have felt when he painted the rectangle. He wondered whether the little loops were part of the original design

~ 190 ~

or an afterthought. One way or another, they were unmistakably meaningful. An entire history, once lost in translation, came into focus.

Rose and Sasha looked incredulously at one another. Todd had prided himself on his pragmatic approach to Max's illness, accusing them of grasping at straws. He had habitually refused to acknowledge that the circles and lines represented his presence in the portraits. Now the tables were turned. He alone understood that the rectangle with handles represented his impending absence. The second portrait lamented the loss of what was so hard-won in the first, a story line culminating in what would amount to abandonment, if he went through with it. In this light, redeployment was an act of cowardice based on the assumption that winning the war on terror abroad was more likely than defeating autism on the home front. The fact that such a complicated emotional matrix could be reduced to such simple terms left little room for evasion. All along, without know it, Todd had been choosing between Afghanistan and his son. Max was calling his bluff, forcing him to make a conscious rather than unconscious decision.

"He's telling a story," Todd said.

It was Rose and Sasha's turn to be skeptical. Moving from literal to figurative representation was one thing, a remarkable developmental feat. But stringing signs and symbols together into a linear narrative was quite another. They had no idea what Todd was talking about until he pointed out the loops. Even then, it took time to piece the story together, let alone understand its myriad implications.

"How do you know they're handles?" Sasha asked.

Todd left the table to fetch his duffel bag from the coat closet. He dragged it across the floor the way Max did, grasping the loop on the end rather than the one in the middle. He hesitated to tell them about Max's epic struggle with the bag. This was between him and Max, the time-honored story of fathers and sons lost and found again. He hesitated to tell them anything at all for fear of colonizing Max's message. The simplicity of his vocabulary in no way precluded multiple meanings. If anything, it inspired a wider spectrum of interpretation. The shapes spoke for themselves. Let Rose and Sasha draw their own conclusions.

*   *   *

Rose found herself wandering around the house a lot. She tried to remember what she used to do with her time before discovering the Source. Virtually nothing came to mind. It was as though her brain had been washed clean, leaving no memory of her former self. Todd was decent enough not to talk about it much. But Rose knew full well he had thought she'd been abducted by Tashi and her cronies. She almost wished it were true. Abduction assumed there was someone to abduct, an authentic identity she might recover now that she wasn't living her life online. Who had she been when she and Todd were first married, before Max's diagnosis? All she knew for sure was that she was still a wife and mother, a set of facts that did very little to help solve the riddle of who she might have been, once upon a time.

Judging from the weeks that had transpired since she last logged on to the Source, she was a devoted housewife who loved, above all, to clean closets and shelves. She wandered around opening doors and cupboards, searching for something. Far from finding anything of value, she felt compelled to throw everything away. The impulse to purge seemed counterproductive, given her need to fill the void left by bogus New Age promises. But her compulsion overwhelmed every other consideration, rational or otherwise. She made short work of the kitchen, jettisoning stale herbs, consolidating stray packages of flax seed and wheat germ, and tossing out unopened staples with lapsed expiration dates, some of which actually predated her abduction. She took this as a sign of how egregiously she had neglected her responsibilities, which fueled her determination to make a clean sweep of the entire house.

Rose knew better than to touch, let alone discard, anything belonging to Max. Todd's stuff was so well-organized, there was nothing expendable, except maybe an odd sock here and a broken gadget there. Maureen was another story entirely. She came home from school to find a pile of clothes next to the recycling bin. Given the general state of their daughter's bedroom, which Todd called a disaster area, Rose assumed she wouldn't miss ratty old clothes that had been balled up in the backs of drawers and closets for years. No exaggeration. But Maureen had her own system, apparently. Underneath her disregard for superficial tidiness, she shared the Barron family's genetic predisposition for order.

"What are all my clothes doing in the garage?" Maureen demanded.

"Not all of them," Rose said. "Just the ones you never wear."

"What are you doing with them?"

"I'm taking them to the Salvation Army."

"They're my favorite."

"You haven't worn them in years, Maureen."

"I'm saving them."

"Saving them for what?"

"So they won't wear out."

"You'll outgrow them before you'll ever wear them out."

"I don't care. They're my favorite and I'm keeping them."

Rose was reminded of Max's outrage when she made the mistake of trying to dispose of Ralph and Harry. She conceded that she had crossed a boundary, which effectively ended the quest to find herself amidst the domestic flotsam and jetsam that is the purview of wives and mothers. But expanding the parameters of her search was easier said than done. At a loss as to where to turn next, she nearly suffered a relapse. She actually logged on to the Source and was one number away from renewing her membership before she hurled her MasterCard across the room. Living life online was no longer an option. At the same time, she couldn't conceive of an alternative without surfing the web. She limited herself to half an hour a day, thirty precious minutes of feverishly looking up listings of local events. She confined her searches to a thirty-mile radius, trying to resist the magnetic pull of the universe, whose abundance masked the black hole that had engulfed her.

Las Vegas and its environs had plenty to offer tourists and rattlesnakes, but not much of interest to Rose. She blamed herself. Without knowing who she was, how could she expect to find anything worthwhile to do? Other people had hobbies. She had an autistic son and an Internet addiction, which had pretty much monopolized her time since his diagnosis. The important thing was to get out. To try new things. First she enrolled in Bikram Yoga classes at the Om on the Range Yoga Center. The clientele reminded her too much of her soul mates, especially Nirvana and Libra, who had been avid Hatha practitioners. Rose was obviously still in the grip of an addiction to New Age fads. Next she tried Pilates, which attracted an entirely different, tonier crowd. She quite liked them until she joined the group for lunch, where all they discussed was getting work done. She thought they were talking about their jobs, not their plastic surgeons, a misunderstanding that inspired her to check out the want ads online. Almost any gainful employment seemed more worthwhile than hobnobbing with ladies with nothing better to do than obsess over crow's feet. But she was really only free from nine to one, the hours Sasha spent with Max. The rest of the day, Rose was still his Floortime facilitator. Even waitressing jobs demanded more flexibility than her commitment to his recovery would allow.

She started to doubt whether she'd ever work again. Not that it bothered her too much one way or the other, as long as she felt fulfilled. Most parents relied on their kids for fulfillment, of course, especially mothers. This had been the source of Rose's biggest mistake. She could no longer afford the luxury of pretending Max would attend a regular grade school in a year or two, counting on New Age fairy tales to alleviate her disappointment in his recovery. Wishful thinking had almost destroyed her marriage. It had placed a terrible burden on her son, as though his progress, or lack thereof, defined her worth. Her need to be absolved of the guilt she felt as his mother stemmed more from intolerance than from love. She kept reminding herself that nothing terrible had happened to Max, nothing she as a parent might have prevented. He didn't have a problem. She did.

Once she let go of her expectations, she noticed a change, one she didn't know whether to attribute to Max or to herself. Either she was simply more accepting of his behavior, or he was actually less distracted lately, not quite so distant. Even when he was in his own little world, that world appeared to intersect with the one she inhabited. He seemed less alien. The idea that he had ever seemed alien at all was something she hadn't dared admit to herself until now. This admission relieved them of the need to pretend otherwise. Once in a while, rather than whipping Max into Floortime frenzies of activity, she would just let him be. They would hang out together, he doing his own thing, she trying to figure out what her own thing might be. He would spend the afternoon straightening the rug fringe while she straightened up the rest of the house. He seemed calmer, somehow. Or she was calmer, especially once she finally found an outlet, something she liked to do as much as he liked twisting each little string until it lay perfectly straight where it belonged.

She discovered it accidentally driving to the farmers' market downtown. The feeder highway was even more jammed than usual, bumper-to-bumper all the way from Sunrise Manor. All the locavores this side of Red Rock Canyon must have been converging on the same few bushels of fresh fruit and vegetables. On second thought, they looked more like tourists en route to some casino matinee, probably David

Copperfield's magic show, judging from the preponderance of comb-overs and blue hair. The assholes in the left lane wouldn't let her merge, and she ended up getting squeezed onto the freeway exit. Once she curved out of the on-ramp, she stepped on the gas. If she didn't hurry, there wouldn't be any raspberries left. She jockeyed into the left lane, leaving several semis and a Cadillac in the dust. The feel of the wheel and the grip of rubber on the road triggered a sense memory. She instinctively rolled down all the windows. Blasts of desert air sent her hair flying in the wind. By the time the exit back to Las Vegas appeared in the rearview mirror, she was pushing eighty. Speed alone precluded returning to Sin City, let alone the fact that there was nothing there for her. Her Taurus kicked into overdrive. It wasn't a Jaguar, but it held its own on the open road. Everything fell into place.

Real driving means driving without a destination. In the desert there is nowhere to go and nothing to see except more of the same. Sagebrush and sagebrush. Mile markers ticked by with incantatory regularity, serving no real function. Distances were too vast to be measured mathematically, an exercise as futile as counting grains of sand to determine the size of a dune, much less the entire Mojave, stretching from Nevada to California with a shaft of road shot from one end to the other, long and straight and true. She measured her momentum against a lone bluff in the distance, what was left of a volcanic cone that lent the landscape a prehistoric improbability. The scale of it all provided a kind of corrective, a way of distancing herself from the narcissistic notion that she was the center of the universe, the source of anything, let alone everything. It had been all about her for too long, as though her pretty little head could change anything, the location of a single sagebrush or the bluff itself, immense, yet barely a blip in the big sky.

Once she reached the open road she never pulled off except to eat and gas up, all at the same lone truck stop at the junction of Interstate 15 and Clark County 215. The first few times she ventured out, she brought a picnic lunch from home, things like hummus and pita and slices of fruit that were easy to eat in transit. But health food on the road felt incongruous, even a little ridiculous, like caviar at a baseball game. Jack's Truck Stop was famous for its double cheeseburgers and super-sized sides of fries. The fact that she hadn't eaten red meat for so long gave her pause. She ordered a Sprite to wash it all down, drawing the line at caffeine. Eventually she caved in completely, abandoning herself to the unadulterated rush of classic Coke. Mustard. Catsup. Extra pickles and minced onions. No wonder they called it relish. The drive-thru girls got to know Rose so well they recognized her Ford at the pump. By the time she finished gassing up, her order was ready and she was back on the road in no time.

Buzzards wheeled overhead, which meant something managed to live in that godforsaken country. Predators had to eat something, after all, nocturnal animals hiding in holes by day and scuttling over the desert floor by night to lick dew drops from parched pebbles. Once in a while Rose spotted one of them, not running for its life but splayed and baking on the pavement. For long stretches of time, roadkill was the only evidence of other drivers. Truckers avoided this stretch of the county highway, which was so far off the beaten track even advertisers had abandoned all hope. Roadside signs were completely effaced by sandstorms, all but one which read, "o opping." This sign took on a strange significance. Its capacity to communicate without fully articulating its message seemed emblematic of something important. *O opping* became a kind of mantra for Rose. They were syllables, not words, signs without sound not unlike Max's hieroglyphic shapes. The more she drove the more she understood that less was more out there. The desert itself was all the more expressive by virtue of its mute minimalism. What was true there might be true everywhere.

One day she thought she might take Todd driving again. She might even show him her sign, though it wouldn't necessarily mean much to him. *O opping.* Any attempt to explain its significance would be futile, at best, a reduction of its meaning to mere words. Let him draw his own conclusions. They would probably stop at one of the motels along the way, just for old times' sake. They would probably laugh at how lame the Taurus was compared to the Jaguar. But speed and wind and the open road were the same, no matter what the trappings. The ineffable allure of driving for the sake of driving was something her husband had always understood implicitly. He was a pilot, after all. Flying was its own raison d'être, too, which is why Rose ultimately accepted Todd's decision to redeploy.

* * *

Todd worried about Farley when orders came down to reassign his drone to the big mission. Surveilling the old couple's hotel had been his sole responsibility for months. Their grandchildren had visited. Birthday and holiday celebrations had come and gone. Clients smoked untold numbers of cigarettes on the communal front porch, and the old man snuck his fair share behind the garden shed, eliciting stormy fights and steamy reconciliations with his wife. Farley was privy to everything, bearing witness to their most intimate interactions. But he showed no signs of missing the old couple. He showed no signs of anything at all, transferring his indefatigable attention to the compound in Abbottabad without skipping a beat. Todd finally realized there was no reason whatsoever to worry about Farley. His detachment wasn't a symptom of some kind of personality disorder that might compromise the big mission. He was, if anything, a model drone pilot, impervious to emotional distractions. Man and machine were melded into a single unfeeling, unblinking eye. Farley was a true new millennial pilot, a human panopticon.

Todd was the one who missed the old couple. In spite of his ability to compartmentalize fear and even empathy, when necessary, he was still a quintessentially twentieth-century air force officer. Geographical distance had not yet fully effected indifference, the inevitable byproduct of drone warfare. He had watched over Farley's shoulder, a kind of backseat driver insinuating himself into the private lives of potential targets who turned out to be people. Hundreds of man-hours and a million dollars of military resources had been expended to assess their threat level. Zero. The hotel was just a hotel. The intelligence Farley had gathered was filed away for future reference, most notably the fact that the old couple's make-up sex was spicier than ever, even after half a century of married life. This intelligence had made a deep impression on Todd. He would never forget the old couple, who seemed emblematic of something important. This same intelligence had made no impression whatsoever on Farley, who saw the couple as nothing more than a potential threat. He was equally detached from the drama of the big mission, in spite of the fact that classified information suggested that the new compound under surveillance was far more than just a compound.

Landing the big mission was a feather in Colonel Trumble's cap. If there had ever been any doubt as to whether he was the most respected commander of RPA combat patrols, this assignment dispelled them. Todd's position in the chain of command was far less certain. He had no way of knowing how many other squads were surveilling Abbottabad, if any. Colonel Trumble wasn't at liberty to discuss the overall tactical operations plan. It was entirely possible that Todd's squad was flying solo, in which case he had been singled out as Colonel Trumble's right-hand man. Evidently, the kerfuffle surrounding his redeployment request hadn't hurt his prospects. All the more reason to expect he would have heard from Central Command by now, one way or the other. He was watching his e-mail almost as assiduously as the compound, still waiting for official word on the status of his application. The suspense was killing him.

He and Colonel Trumble talked several times a day now, but neither one of them ever mentioned Todd's predicament. The task at hand precluded digressions of any kind, with the notable exception of the colonel's irrepressible wisecracks. A special communications system had been installed in the trailer, a hotline connecting Todd with a network of undisclosed agencies under the jurisdiction of an undisclosed command. The big mission, or the BM as Colonel Trumble liked to call it, was so top secret even Todd wasn't privy to the target's identity. The level of surveillance suggested it was one of al Qaeda's top brass, hiding in plain sight. A less likely safe house was inconceivable, given the compound's central location. Hunters in the squad likened it to a duck blind.

"This is one big piece of shit, I can tell you that," Colonel Trumble said.

"Yes, Sir," Todd said.

"It's time to pull the plug, if you ask me."

"Yes, Sir."

"The way I see it, we have two options. Flush first, or just wipe him out."

"Sir?"

"Send in the SEALs, or just bomb the hell out of the place. What do you think?"

"Your call, Sir."

"I wish."

The fact that Colonel Trumble could get away with this kind of gutter talk was a testament to his stature. He was like General Grant, boozing his way through the war with impunity as long as he kicked Lee's ass. The colonel's scatological humor put Todd in an awkward position. He couldn't really respond in kind the way he did when they were hobnobbing in person. Every word they uttered was being recorded and monitored by a network of military and intelligence agencies, including the Pentagon, the CIA, possibly even the White

House. Once in a while Todd thought he heard muffled laughter on the line, presumably one of the masterminds of the BM. Apparently, you could laugh all you liked at the top of the pecking order. No doubt Colonel Trumble consulted with them, but only after Todd signed off. He called them Roto-Rooter Men, the counterterrorism strategists responsible for flushing out the al Qaeda pipeline.

"A shit this big can plug up the works, if you're not careful."

"Yes, Sir."

"Anything new on your end, Barron?"

"A suspicious number of early morning deliveries. I'm not convinced the baker is just a baker."

"Awfully damn skinny for a baker, that's for sure."

"This is the second time this week he's delivered a big cake box, along with the usual order of naan. When I say big I mean really big. Nobody eats that much cake."

"Unless there's more people in that compound than meets the eye."

"Unless there's more in those boxes than meets the eye."

"How big is big?"

"Big enough to disguise several cartridges of ammunition. Maybe even grenades."

"Any corroborating evidence? Or are you boys just making shit up because you're bored?"

"This particular bakery seems to have an awful lot of employees, especially since it's basically a mom and pop shop. We're monitoring it 24/7."

Todd's drone squad was responsible for providing real-time video feeds documenting traffic in and out of the compound. The hotline was reserved for reporting anomalies in the daily routine of its inhabitants. There was one main house, a bland two-story box with balconies, and two outbuildings, which could have accommodated up to twenty people, if need be. A lot of space was being wasted, or not, depending on whether anyone was hiding behind closed doors. Not that it was an inordinately large compound. It basically looked like the homes of other wealthy people living nearby. The grounds were surrounded by a twelve-foot concrete wall laced with barbed wire, neither more nor less heavily fortified than neighboring properties. These were standard precautions in Abbottabad, no more out of the way than locking your door in Las Vegas. The primary and quite possibly only residents appeared to be a couple in their late fifties, along with a battery of domestic servants. The husband, who had an office downtown, made his money trading credit derivatives. The wife was either an invalid, agoraphobic, or just too devout to venture into public. Four out of their five grown children lived locally and visited regularly. The fifth and eldest flew in from Karachi for religious holidays. Three were married and one was pregnant, praise Allah. Late fifties was a decidedly advanced age to become grandparents in Abbottabad.

The couple was either fronting a terrorist cell or they were the object of an egregious invasion of privacy. There was very little in their background indicating that they were more apt to harbor al Qaeda operatives than their neighbors, which begged the question of whether Pakistan was crawling with collaborators. Homeland Security advisers were divided on the subject. One camp felt that the escalation in surveillance, let alone drone strikes, had alienated the general public, fanning the fire of terrorism. The other, including most of the Joint Chiefs, insisted that Pakistanis had been dubious allies all along, well before drones invaded their airspace. Whether this kind of surveillance was ever really justified was another question entirely, one the intelligence community was singularly ill-equipped to answer. You might as well ask a watchdog why it barks. The more immediate problem—deciding whether this particular couple's compound was a viable target—far exceeded the question of whether they were guilty as charged. What was really on trial was American foreign policy, which was completely irrelevant to Todd's squad. They were trained to follow orders, not ask questions.

Each of Todd's pilots had been assigned to monitor very specific areas and activities. Brown and Farley's sensors kept their eyes on the prize, never venturing beyond the confines of the compound. Once a visitor was buzzed through the electronic gate, they were added to a CIA list of suspected terrorists. Franklin and Kucher were responsible for surveilling their movements once they left the premises. Counterterrorism agents, preferably turncoat Pakistanis, were recruited to follow them into places drone sensors couldn't penetrate without recourse to X-ray technology, which was still in early stages of development. Double agents were particularly valuable, one of whom managed to land a job as the receptionist for the couple's internist, whose frequent house calls corroborated the theory that the wife was, in fact, an invalid. A nurse practitioner by trade, the hope was that this agent would eventually be promoted, thereby gaining access to the compound in the event that the wife suffered a medical crisis requiring overnight surveillance. In the meantime, the doctor himself had dropped hints that he might be willing to leak information, provided the price was right. The noose was tightening around the compound.

The Roto-Rooter Men were like chess masters mapping out moves. Every possible scenario was followed to its logical conclusion, generating thousands of contingency plans. The level of detail was staggering. The danger of such close scrutiny was not seeing the forest for the trees. To offset this threat, Poindexter's drone hovered over the entire region, monitoring the activities of the town in general. An awful lot of traffic came in and out of Abbottabad. Every single license plate was plugged into a central intelligence database, a clearinghouse for all manner of suspicious vehicles. Compared to other cities with the same population profile, far fewer questionable cars and trucks showed up on the registry. This fact tended to raise rather than lower the odds that Abbottabad was harboring al Qaeda operatives. Assuming their transportation networks were capable of such high levels of organization, care was being taken to deflect attention away from the area. The plot thickened.

One particular aspect of the BM blew Todd's mind, and it wasn't even classified information. Tucked in the Orash Valley in the Himalayan foothills, Abbottabad's natural beauty made it a favorite home for retired military personnel. Never mind the fact that the Pakistan Military Academy was four miles away in Kakul. He couldn't decide whether these factors made it more or less likely that al Qaeda muckety-mucks would choose this precise location to hole up, rather than some cozy little cave in the Karakoram Mountains. If the surveillance target was a real target, he was getting cocky, either out of complacency or the conviction that retired army officers provided a safer haven than tribal hideouts, no matter how remote. Assuming the Pakistan military was complicit, the politics surrounding this particular targeted assassination were even more fraught than usual. Todd tried not to think about it. Washington was responsible for determining whether drone strikes were counterproductive, inciting the very resistance they were meant to quell. He was just in charge of pulling the trigger, not calling the shots.

Todd spent most of his time floating from one virtual cockpit to another, trying to take in the big picture while simultaneously keeping track of relevant details. He had to force himself to check in on Franklin, Kucher, and Poindexter. Even though these three covered far more ground, providing wide-ranging points of interest, Todd gravitated to Brown and Farley's monitors, which never strayed from the target. Something about the compound mesmerized him. It certainly wasn't the architecture. The main building in particular was almost ugly, a white cube in need of a paint job, with nothing to recommend it but wraparound balconies. Privacy walls all but obscured the view, making it impossible to look out without standing up. The husband never appeared without a drink in his hand, usually scotch on the rocks. His wife almost never appeared at all. When she did, usually early in the morning, her hijab concealed her even more completely than the walls. If they knew they were being watched, they betrayed no signs of it. They never touched one another, at least not outside, but neither did their neighbors. Nothing whatever in their behavior set them apart, yet Todd was riveted.

He had a feeling about the compound, just as he had formerly had a feeling about the old couple's hotel. He couldn't put his finger on it. There had been no real way to confirm that the hotel was just a hotel. Yet he had known it all along. This compound was like a seething volcano in comparison, biding its time until the next 9/11. Its inevitability was the true source of terror, much more so than the actual eruption, which would be over long before fallout finished spreading paranoia from sea to shining sea. This foreboding made it difficult for Todd to file prudent reports. The challenge was to avoid equally disastrous extremes in judgment, crying wolf on the one hand and underestimating the importance of suspicious anomalies on the other. Unusual amounts of garbage. Lights left on well after the couple went to bed. It didn't help that Colonel Trumble was uncharacteristically trigger-happy. The pressure to provide incriminating evidence was relentless.

"It's time to shit or get off the pot," Colonel Trumble said.

"Yes, Sir."

"The longer we fart around, the more likely the target will relocate."

"No chance of that, Sir. Not unless he can fit into a cake box."

Most of the intelligence gathered by Todd's squad came from Brown. Nothing escaped his notice. Handwritten letters smoldering in the incinerator. A pair of shutters that never opened, even during family visits. He obviously understood that this wasn't just another routine surveillance mission. The more the colonel pressured Todd, the more he relied on Brown's infallible eye. They never talked about it, of course, not even when they went rock climbing. But they finally felt like they were really contributing, not sitting on the sidelines. At the same time, Todd wondered if he wasn't kidding himself, hyping the importance of the BM in case he wound up staying in Nevada instead of deploying to Afghanistan. Given the timing of this top secret assignment, he was pretty sure the powers that be had already decided his fate. Even so, he was almost afraid to click on the e-mail when it finally showed up in his inbox.

> *Per your request, your petition for deployment has been withdrawn. You are hereby authorized to maintain your current assignment at Creech AFB until further notice.*

He thought he was mentally prepared for any eventuality. In the event that he wasn't, he could rely on his training to maintain his equilibrium, at least until his shift was over. The effort was exhausting.

He wanted to call Rose with the news, but the colonel kept badgering him on the hotline. Even the heightened drama of the BM couldn't eclipse a barrage of emotions ranging from relief to a nagging sense of guilt. He felt good about choosing his family over the thrill of another deployment. But doing the right thing at home seemed to preclude doing the right thing abroad. For all its alleged surgical precision, drone warfare posed ethical questions Todd still couldn't answer. Putting your life on the line in combat seemed like the only surefire way to justify taking the lives of others, something soldiers understood as well as civilians back in the day when there was a clear distinction between the two. But now that the option of redeploying was no longer on the table, he needed to silence his qualms. A consummate professional, he compartmentalized reservations that jeopardized the success of the mission, trusting the mission itself wouldn't spawn more terrorists than it killed.

* * *

Todd pulled into the driveway and started closing the windows. Then he opened them back up again. Something smelled way too good to be true. He assumed his neighbor Fred was barbecuing steaks. When Rose wasn't around, Todd stationed himself next to the fence, breathing in the delicious smoke from Fred's grill. It was a kind of olfactory voyeurism, innocent enough as long as nobody knew about it. He ran around back, half expecting to see Rose wielding a fire extinguisher, beating back the offending flames. Wonders will never cease. Sure enough, there was Rose. But she had tongs in her hand and she was barbecuing ribs and corn on the cob.

"Hi Todd," she said. "Hungry?"

He was speechless. Someone must have abducted his wife, the New Age macrobiotic health nut. The alien chef masquerading as Rose was obviously amused by his reaction.

"Could you take over here?" she asked. "I've got stuff on the stove."

Rose handed him the tongs and went inside, as though they were just another family barbecuing ribs and corn. Good thing grilling was like riding a bike. It had been awhile. Twenty-three and a half months to be exact, but who's counting? Todd particularly enjoyed the symmetrical challenge of barbecuing ribs. You couldn't just fire up the briquettes, line them up, and call it a day. The secret to savory, mouth-watering ribs was in the grid. Todd had developed a complex, kinetic configuration to guarantee that the outside rib joints cooked as much as the inside ones, just enough to make them fall off the bone. This required rotating each rib row, first clockwise then counterclockwise, keeping meticulous track of their relative proximity to the vortex of heat. The center of the grill was the sweet spot. In keeping with the gastronomical, if not existential, golden rule, too much of a good thing spoiled even the most perfectly marinated meats.

Todd was almost embarrassed to admit how unspeakably happy he was at that moment. He felt like a king, a suburban monarch wielding his diadem tongs. To say that Rose's vegan regime had emasculated him was ridiculous. Surely they had evolved beyond the Neanderthal habit of equating meat with masculinity. It was more about pleasure than gender. Pure pleasure. Rose had been punishing herself for something. For the past two years, all roads seemed to lead to the same something: Max's diagnosis. Tofu was a form of penance, kombu a kind of flagellation of the gustatory senses. The long exculpatory fast was over. Max could be autistic without the entire family having to suffer for it.

Maureen came tripping out the back door, laden with napkins and paper plates.

"Hi Dad."

"Pretty exciting, huh?"

"What?"

"Dinner."

"We're having chocolate cupcakes for dessert."

"You're kidding."

"With ice cream."

"When was the last time we had ice cream?"

"I have it all the time. Over at Leslie's."

Maureen sprawled across the picnic table, setting places from a prone position to avoid having to walk around its perimeter. The results were haphazard, at best. Todd never ceased to marvel at the profound difference between their two children, at polar opposite ends of the spectrum spanning the meticulous to the messy. The fact that only one extreme was considered pathological seemed unfair. Half the time, Maureen's chaotic habits drove him crazier than Max's devotion to order.

He rotated the ribs 120 degrees counterclockwise. The corn was cooked, so he shunted it off to the side to keep warm.

"Tell your mother we're almost finished out here," Todd said.

"We're almost finished out here," Maureen yelled. She trundled over to the hammock and climbed in.

The screen door slammed and there was Rose, carrying a big bowl of macaroni salad. Todd was practically dizzy with anticipation. Rose continued to act like they were just like everyone else, a happy family enjoying a midweek barbecue. Then it occurred to Todd that they weren't just acting anymore.

"Maureen," Rose said. "Tell Max dinner is ready."

"He won't listen," Maureen said from the hammock.

"Then just bring him outside. The way Sasha taught you."

Todd arranged the ribs and corn on a platter. He opted for a kind of checkerboard pattern he thought Max might like. Rose slammed back in and out of the screen door carrying a bowl of potatoes and a pitcher of lemonade. Maureen negotiated the door more carefully, clutching one end of a jump rope with Max tagging along on the other. This way they could hold hands without actually touching, a level of intimacy Max could tolerate. She opened the screen with her foot and then eased it shut so it wouldn't startle him. Todd had never seen her be so careful with anything, except maybe her toenail polish. They all sat down and started helping themselves, with the notable exception of Max. He stared at the round bowl filled with round, tan potatoes while Rose dished up his plate.

Todd almost wept when he tasted his first bite of ribs. For real. He felt like he'd gotten his life back, something he realized only then he'd given up for lost. The ribs were slathered with barbecue sauce. The macaroni salad was slathered with mayonnaise. The corn was slathered with butter. Now this was what he called eating.

Rose looked tentative at first, like she was dipping her big toe into a huge vat of saturated fat that might swallow her up if she weren't careful. But even she couldn't resist the allure of the macaroni salad, the ultimate comfort food. When she reached for the salt shaker—iodized rather than sea salt, for once—Todd took her hand in his. Cholesterol be damned, this was love.

Maureen was inhaling her dinner, as usual, to get to dessert as quickly as possible. Max was lining up his potatoes in two rows of four. He had pushed his corn and ribs to the side without bothering to fling them from his plate. Either he was making progress or they were linear enough to meet his criteria of acceptable shapes. One of his rows was complete. The second was two potatoes shy of being perfect. Inconceivably, Rose had served him six rather than eight potatoes. His face registered unspeakable terror, which Todd noticed just in time. He spooned two more onto Max's plate, and the crisis was averted.

"What were you thinking?" Todd asked.

"Must have been distracted," Rose said. She gave him one of those guess-what's-for-dessert looks, turning her head so that Maureen couldn't see. Apparently the adults were having more than just ice cream with their chocolate cupcakes.

Todd sat back to take in the glory of it all before serving himself seconds of everything. This was it, the moment that made it all worthwhile. His sexy wife oversalting her food. His autistic son serenely lining up his potatoes. Even his daughter seemed to be living in the moment, enjoying her corn rather than focusing exclusively on the promise of chocolate things to come. She flashed him a big smile with what looked like an entire ear stuck between her teeth. He wanted to say something meaningful, to commemorate the occasion. Language failed him again. Words couldn't possibly capture what he was feeling. No big loss. They would just break the spell anyway.

"Pass the potatoes, please," Todd finally managed to say.

Maureen shoved them across the table, almost upsetting the bowl. Todd spooned eight potatoes onto his plate. He finished the first row of four by the time anyone noticed what he was doing.

"Don't encourage him," Rose said.

"They taste better this way," Todd said.

Maureen laughed so hard she choked on a rib. "Pass the potatoes," she said when she recovered.

"Please," Rose said.

"Please."

There were only six potatoes left so Maureen had to improvise. For the sake of symmetry, she opted for two rows of three.

Rose looked from one plate to the next. This was the fruit of all her labors of love, the way her husband and children spent quality time together. Max's potatoes were the most perfectly aligned, but Todd's were a close second. Maureen's configuration looked more like controlled chaos than actual order. But she had made the effort. A family that stims together stays together.

"Don't knock it till you've tried it," Todd said.

Fortunately, Rose still had four potatoes left, all bunched together in the center of her plate. She scraped her rib bones onto a side dish to give herself room to maneuver. Two rows of two would have formed a square, which was completely unacceptable. She prodded her potatoes into a single, elegant row of four. She used a spoon instead of a fork to avoid puncturing them. Her spacing was impeccable.

When everyone's potatoes were lined up like so many ducks in a row, they looked at Max, if not for approval then for something, anything. He was staring, they thought, at nothing in particular. His peripheral vision included the rectangular table and the round grill. Suddenly he started clapping his hands. Todd was the first to respond. Then they all clapped with him. Something was better than nothing.